William Henry Frost

Fairies and Folk of Ireland

William Henry Frost

Fairies and Folk of Ireland

ISBN/EAN: 9783944349084

Auflage: 1

Erscheinungsjahr: 2013

Erscheinungsort: Bremen, Deutschland

CONTENTS

SHOULD YOU ASK ME, WHENCE THESE STORIES?"

The story which runs through and makes up the bulk of this book is my own. The intention has been, however, to make it conform to the laws governing certain beings commonly regarded in this country as mythical, as those laws are revealed in the folk-lore of many peoples, and particularly of the Irish people. Almost every incident in which the fairies are concerned might occur, and very many of them do actually occur, in Irish folk-lore. But in a real folk-tale there are usually only two or three, or, at any rate, only a few, of the characteristic incidents, while this story attempts to combine many of them.

The shorter stories wherewith the main story is interspersed are all, to the best of my information and belief, genuine Irish folk-tales. I have told them in my own way, of course. I have sometimes condensed and sometimes elaborated them, but I have seldom, if ever, I think, materially changed their substance. I have never had the opportunity to collect such stories as these for myself, and if I had, I should probably find that I had not the ability. I have therefore had to turn for the substance of these tales to collections made by others — men whose patient and affectionate care and labor have preserved a great mass of the beautiful Irish legends, which, without them, might have died.

It seems hardly right to give to any one of these collectors a preference over the others by naming him first. But when I count up my indebtedness, I find that the book to which I owe more stories than to any other is Patrick Kennedy's "Legendary Fictions of the Irish Celts." From this book I have borrowed, as to their substance, the story of Earl Gerald, in Chapter II. of my own book; the story of the children of Lir, in the same chapter; the account of the changeling who was tempted by the bagpipes, which Naggeneen tells of himself, in Chapter V.; the changeling story which Mrs. O'Brien tells, in Chapter VI.; and the most of the story of Oisin, in Chapter IX., besides part of the story of the fairies' tune, in Chapter VII. With respect to Oisin I got a little help from an article on "The Neo-Latin Fay," by Henry Charles Coote, in "The Folk-Lore Record," Vol. II. The story of the fairies' tune is in part derived from T. Crofton Croker's "Fairy Legends and Traditions of the South of Ireland." This delightful book as well deserves the first place in my list as does Kennedy's, for it gave me one of my most important stories, that of O'Donoghue, in Chapter I., and it gave me Naggeneen. Him I first saw, with Mr. Croker's help, sitting on the cask of port in the cellar of old MacCarthy of Ballinacarthy, as he himself describes in Chapter II. It is not enough to say that after that he came readily into my story; he simply could not be kept out of it. The tale of the fairies who wanted to question a priest, in Chapter X., is also from Croker. Mrs. O'Brien's method of getting rid of a changeling is founded on one of Croker's stories, and a story almost exactly like it is told by Grimm. There is also a form of it in Brittany. Two books by W.B. Yeats have been of much value — "Irish Fairy and Folk Tales" and "The Celtic Twilight." Of the former Mr. Yeats is the editor, rather than, in a strict sense, the author, though it contains some of his own work, and his introduction, notes, and other comments are of great interest. From this book I have the story of Hudden, Dudden, and Donald, in Chapter VII. Mr. Yeats reproduces it from an old chap-book. A version of it is also found in Samuel Lover's "Legends and Stories of Ireland." Those who like to compare the stories which they find in various places will not fail to note its likeness to Hans Christian Andersen's "Big Claus and Little Claus." The story of the monk and the bird, in Chapter IX., Mr. Yeats reproduces from Croker, though not from the work of his which has already been mentioned. I could not resist the temptation to better the story, as I thought, by the addition of an incident from a German version of it, and everybody will remember the beautiful form in which it appears in Longfellow's "The Golden Legend." From Mr. Yeats's "The Celtic Twilight" I have the little story of the conversation between the diver and the conger, in Chapter II. It is a pleasure to refer to two such fine and scholarly works as Dr. Douglas Hyde's "Beside the Fire" and William Larminie's "West Irish Folk-Tales and Romances." From the former of these I have borrowed the substance of the story of Guleesh na Guss Dhu, in Chapter IV., and from the latter that of the ghost and his wives, in Chapter VII.

Having thus confessed my indebtedness, it would seem that my next duty was to pay it. I fear that I can pay it only with thanks. I have not taken a story from the work of any living collector without his permission. It thus becomes my pleasure, no less than my duty, to express my gratitude to Mr. Yeats for permission to use the stories in "Irish Fairy and Folk Tales" and "The Celtic Twilight;" to Dr. Hyde for his permission to take what I chose from "Beside the Fire," and to Mr. Larminie and his publisher, Elliott Stock, for the same permission with regard to his "West Irish Folk-Tales and Romances." My thanks are equally due to Macmillan & Co., Limited, for permission to take stories from Kennedy's "Legendary Fictions of the Irish Celts," the rights to which they own. I wish to say also that in each of these cases the permission asked has been given with a readiness and a cordiality no less pleasing than the permission itself.

I have learned much concerning the ways of Irish fairies from Lady Wilde's "Ancient Legends, Mystic Charms, and Superstitions of Ireland" and "Ancient Cures, Charms, and Usages of Ireland," and I have gained not a little from the books of William Carleton, especially his "Traits and Stories of the Irish Peasantry," but from none of these have I taken any considerable part of a story. Indeed I have found help, greater or less, in more books than I can name here.

It may seem by this time that I am like the lawyer who conceded this and that to his opponent till the judge said: "Do not concede any more; you conceded your whole case long ago." But I have not conceded my whole case. I have used the threads which others have spun, but I have done my own weaving. The shorter stories have been told before, but they have never been put together in this way before, and, as I said at first, the main story is my own.

W.H.F.

New York, September 1, 1900.

FAIRIES AND FOLK OF IRELAND

I.
O'DONOGHUE

It was in a poor little cabin somewhere in Ireland. It does not matter where. The walls were of rough stone, the roof was of thatch, and the floor was the hard earth. There was very little furniture. Poor as it was, the whole place was clean. It is right to tell this, because, unhappily, a good many cabins in Ireland are not clean. What furniture there was had been rubbed smooth and spotless, and the few dishes that there were fairly shone. The floor was as carefully swept as if the Queen were expected.

The three persons who lived in the cabin had eaten their supper of potatoes and milk and were sitting before the turf fire. It had been a poor supper, yet a little of it that was left — a few potatoes, a little milk, and a dish of fresh water — had been placed on a bench outside the door. There was no light except that of the fire. There was no need of any other, and there was no money to spend on candles that were not needed.

The three who sat before the fire, and needed no other light, were a young man, a young woman, and an elderly woman. She did not like to be called old, for she said, and quite truly, that sixty was not old for anybody who felt as young as she did. This woman was Mrs. O'Brien. The young man was her son, John, and the young-woman was his wife, Kitty.

"Kitty," said John, "it's not well you're lookin' to-night. Are ye feelin' anyways worse than common?"

"It's only a bit tired I am," said Kitty, "wid the work I was afther doin' all day. I'll be as well as ever in the morning."

"It's a shame, that it is," said John, "that ye have to be workin' that way, day afther day, and you not sthrong at all. It's a shame that I can't do enough for the three of us, and the more, maybe, that there'll be, but you must be at it, too, all the time."

"What nonsinse ye're talkin', John," Kitty answered. "What would I be doin', settin' up here like a lady, doin' nothin', and you and mother workin' away like you was my servants? Did you think it was a duchess or the daughter of the Lord Lieutenant ye was marryin', that ye're talkin' that way?"

"And it'll be worse a long time before it's betther," John went on. "Wid the three of us workin' all the time, we just barely get along. And it's the end of the summer now. What we'll do at all when the winter comes, I dunno."

The older woman listened to the others and said nothing. Perhaps she had heard such talk as this so many times that she did not care to join in it again, or perhaps she was waiting to be asked to speak. For it was to her that these younger people always turned when they were in trouble. It was her advice and her opinion that they always asked when they felt that they needed a better opinion than their own. The three sat silent now for a time, and then John broke out, as if the talk had been going on in his mind all the while: "What's the good of us tryin' to live at all?' he said. "Is livin' any use to us? We do nothin' but work all day, and eat a little to give us the strength to work the next day, and then we sleep all night, if we can sleep. And it's that and nothing else all the year through. Are we any better when the year ends than we were when it began? If we've paid the rent, we've done well. We never do more."

"John," the old woman answered, "it's not for us to say why we're here or what for we're living. It's God that put us here, and He'll keep us here till it's our time to go. He has made it the way of all His creatures to provide for themselves and for their own, and to keep themselves alive while they can. When He's ready for us to die, we die. That's all we know. The rest is with Him."

"I know all that's true, mother," said John; "but what is there for us to hope for, that we'ld wish to live? It's nothing but work to keep the roof over us. We don't even eat for any pleasure that's in it — only so that we can work. If we rested for a day, we'ld be driven out of our house. If we rested for another day, we'ld starve. Is there any good to be hoped for such as us? Will there ever be any good times for Ireland? I mean for all the people in it."

"There will," the old woman said. "Everything has an end, and so these troubles of ours will end, and all the troubles of Ireland will end, too."

"And why should we believe that?" John asked again. "Wasn't Ireland always the poor, unhappy country, and all the people in it, only the landlords and the agents, and why should we think it will ever be better?"

"Everything has an end," the old woman repeated. "Ireland was not always the unhappy country. It was happy once and it will be happy again. It's not you, John O'Brien, that ought to be forgetting the good days of Ireland, long ago though they were. For you yourself are the descendant of King Brian Boru, and you know well, for it's many times I've told you, how in his days the country was happy and peaceful and blessed. He drove out the heathen and saved the country for his people. He had strict laws, and the people obeyed them. In his days a lovely girl, dressed all in fine silk and gold and jewels, walked alone the length of Ireland, and there was no one to rob her or to harm her, because of the good King and the love the people had for him and for his laws. And you, that are descended from King Brian, ask if Ireland wasn't always the poor, unhappy country."

"But all that was so long ago," said John; "near a thousand years, was it not? Since then it's been nothing but sorrow for the country and for the people. What good is it to us that the country was happy in King Brian's time? Will that help us pay the rent? And how we'll pay the rent when the winter comes, I dunno, and if we don't pay it we'll be evicted."

"Shaun," said his mother, calling him by the Irish name that she used sometimes — "Shaun, we'll not be evicted; never fear that. Things are bad, and they may be worse, but take my word, whatever comes, we'll not be evicted."

"Mother," said the young man, "you never spoke the word, so far as I know, that wasn't true, but I dunno how it'll be this time. We've been workin' all we can and we only just manage to pay the rent and live, and here's the summer over and the winter coming, and how will we pay the rent then?"

The mother did not answer this question directly. She began talking in a way that did not seem to have anything to do with the rent, though it really had something to do with it, in her own mind, and perhaps in her son's mind too.

"It's over-tired that you are with your hard day's work, Shaun," she said, "and that and seeing Kitty so tired, too, has maybe made you look at things a little worse than they are. We've never been so bad off as many of our neighbors; you know that. And yet I know it's been worse of late and harder for you than it might have been, and you can't remember the better times that our family had, and that's why you forget that the times were ever better. No, you wasn't born then, but the time was when good luck seemed to follow your father and me everywhere and always. Yes, and the good luck has not all left us yet, though we had the bad luck to lose your father so long ago. We could not hope to be rich or happy while the whole country was in such distress as it's been sometimes, yet there were always many that were worse off than we, and when I think of those days of '47 and '48 it makes the sorrows seem light that we're suffering now. And I always know that whatever comes, there'll be some good for me and mine while I live. I've told you how I know that, but you always forget, and I must tell you again."

They had not forgotten. They knew the story that was coming by heart, but they knew that the old woman liked to tell it, so they let her go on and said not a word.

For a little while, too, the old woman said not a word. She sat with her eyes closed, and smiling, as if she were in a dream. Then she began to speak softly, as if she were still only just waking out of a dream. "Blessed days there were," she said — "blessed days for Ireland once — long ago — many hundreds of years. O'Donoghue — it was he was the good King, and happy were his people. A fierce warrior he was to guard them from their enemies, and a just ruler to those who minded his laws. It was in the West that he ruled, by the beautiful Lakes of Killarney. The rich and the poor among his people were alike in one thing — they all had justice. He punished even his own son when he did wrong, as if he had been a poor man and a stranger.

"'BLESSED DAYS THERE WERE,' SHE SAID."

"He gave grand feasts to his friends, and the greatest and the best men of all Erin came to sit at his table and to hear the wise words that he spoke. And the greatest bards of all Erin came to sing before him and his guests of the brave deeds of the heroes of old days and of the greatness and the goodness of O'Donoghue himself. At one of these feasts, after a bard had been singing of the noble days of Erin long ago, O'Donoghue began to speak of the years that were to come for Ireland. He told of much good and of much evil. He told how true and brave and noble men would live and work and fight and die for their country, and how cowards would betray her. He told of glory and he told of shame. He spoke of riches and honor, and poetry and beauty; he spoke of want and disgrace, and degradation and sorrow.

"Those who sat at his table listened to him in wonder. Sometimes their hearts swelled with pride at the noble lives and deeds of those who were to come after them, sometimes they wept at the sufferings that their children were to feel, and sometimes they hid their faces from each other in shame at the tales of cowardice and of treachery.

9

"As he finished speaking he rose from the table, crossed the hall, and walked out at the door and down to the shore of the lake. The others followed him and watched him, full of wonder. They saw him go to the edge of the lake and then walk out upon it, as if the water had been firm ground under his feet. He walked far and far out on the bright lake as they stood and gazed at him. Then he turned toward them, he waved his hand in farewell, and he was gone. They saw him no more."

The old woman paused for a moment and the dreaming look came back to her face. Then she went on. "They saw him no more — but others saw him — and I have seen him. Every year, on the 1st of May, just as the sun is rising, he rides across the lake on his beautiful white horse. He is not always seen, but sometimes a few can see him. And it always brings good luck to see O'Donoghue riding across the lake on May morning. And I saw him."

Again there was a pause, but she had no look of dreaming now. Her eyes were open and she seemed to be looking at something wonderful and beautiful that was far off. Slowly and softly she began speaking again. "I was a girl then. My father lived by the Lakes of Killarney. On that May morning I was standing at the door as the sun was rising. I was looking out upon the lake, far away to the east. The first that I saw was that the water, far off toward the sun, was ruffled, and then all at once a great, white-crested wave rose, as if a strong wind had struck the water, only all the air was still, and no wind ever raises such a wave as that on the lake. The wave came swiftly toward me, and I drew back, in a kind of dread, though I knew that it could not reach me where I stood. But still I looked — and then I saw him.

"Through the flying water and foam and mist I saw the old King, on his white horse, following the great wave across the lake. The sun made all his armor gleam like the silver of the lake itself, and the plume of his helmet streamed away behind him like the spray that a strong wind blows back from the crest of a breaker. After him came a train of glowing, beautiful forms — spirits of the lake or of the air, or some of the Good People — I do not know. They wore soft, flowing garments, that were like the morning mists; they carried chains of pearls and they scattered other pearls about them, that glistened like the drops of a shower when the sun is shining through it. They had garlands of flowers, and they plucked the flowers out and threw them high in the air, so that they fell before the King. They looked like flecks of foam from the waves, turned rosy and violet by the rising sun, but they were flowers. And there was a sound of sweet, soft music, like harps and mellow horns.

"The King and his train came nearer and I saw them plainer, and the music sounded louder. Then they passed me and moved far away again on the lake. The sight of them grew dim and the music grew faint, and I strained my eyes and my ears for the last of them, and they were gone. Then I could move and speak and breathe again, for it had seemed to me that I could not do any one of these things while the King was passing, and I knew that I had seen O'Donoghue."

The old woman stopped, as if the story were ended, but the younger people did not speak, for they knew that she had something else to tell. "O'Donoghue had passed and was gone," she said, "but he always leaves good luck behind him, and he left the good luck with me. That summer some rich young ladies came from Dublin to see the Lakes of Killarney. They heard the story of O'Donoghue, and the people told them that I was the last who had seen him. They came to my father's house and asked me to tell them what I had seen. They seemed pleased with what I told them, or with something that they saw in me, and they asked my father to let them take me back to the city with them, for a lady's maid. He did not like to let me go, but they said that they would pay me well and would have me taught better than I could be at home. He was poor, there were others at home who needed all that he could earn, I wished to go, and at last he said I might.

"So I went to Dublin and lived in a grand house, among grand people. I tried to do my duties well, and they were kind to me. They kept the promise that they had made to my father. They gave me books and allowed me time to study them, and they helped me in things that I could not well have learned by myself, even with the books. I was quick at study, and in the little time that I had, I learned all that I could. Three times they took me to

London with them, and I saw still grander people and grander life.

"Those were happy days, but happier came. Your father came, Shaun. He was a servant of the family, like myself — a coachman. But he was wiser than I, and he talked with me and showed me that there was something better for us than to be servants always. We saved all the money that we could, and when we had enough we came here, where your father had lived before, and took a little farm. The luck of O'Donoghue was always with us. We had a good landlord, who asked a fair rent. We both worked hard, we saved more money and took more land, and all our neighbors thought that we were prosperous, and so we were.

"Then came '47. Nobody could be prosperous then. Nobody that had a heart in him at all could even keep what he had saved then. What we had and what our neighbors had belonged to all, and little enough there was of it. It is well for you young people to talk of these times being hard. Harder than some they may be, but good and easy compared with those days of '47 and '48. You talk of injustice and wrong to Ireland! What think you of those times, when every day great ships sailed away from Ireland loaded down with food — corn and bacon, and beef and butter — and Ireland's own people left without the bit of food to keep the life in them? All summer long was the horrible wet weather, and the potatoes rotting in the ground before they'ld be ripe, and never fit to eat. To add to all that was the fever, that killed its thousands, and then the cold. And when the days came again that the crops would grow, many and many of the people were so weak with the hunger and the sickness that they could not work in the fields. Ah! and you call these hard times!

"Those were the bad days for Ireland, those days of '47. Not even the luck of O'Donoghue could make us prosper or give us comforts then. But we lived through the time, as many others did. The poor helped those who were poorer than themselves; the sick tended those who were sicker; the cold gave clothes and fire to those who were colder. The little money that we had saved helped us and some of our neighbors. And we lived through it all.

"Better times came, though never again so good as the old. We worked again and we saved a trifle. Then you were born to us, John. We had a worse landlord now. He was of the kind that cared nothing for his tenants and nothing for his land, but to get the last penny off it. The rent was raised, and we never could have paid it but for the care and the skill and the hard work of your father. And then, John, you know that when you were hardly old enough to take his place with the work, let alone knowing how to work as well as he, he died and left us — Heaven rest his soul!"

For a long time the old woman said no more, and neither of the others spoke. Then she said: "John, the country is in trouble enough and the times are hard enough for you and for Kitty, here, and for all of us, I know. But don't be cast down. There have been worse days than these; there have been better days, too, and there will be better again."

II.
THE BIG POOR PEOPLE

There was a knock at the door, and John opened it. "God save all here except the cat!" said a voice outside.

"God save you kindly!" John answered.

A young man and a young woman came in. They were neighbors — Peter Sullivan and his wife, Ellen. "Good avenin' to you, Pether," said John; "you're lookin' fine and hearty, and it's like a rose you're lookin', Ellen."

"It's more like nettles than roses we're feelin'," Ellen answered, "but something with prickles anyway, wid the bother we have every day and all day."

"Thrue for you, it's hard times," said John; "we was speaking about them just the minute before you came in; but we all have to bear them. It's not you ought to complain, as long as you've good health; now here's Kitty — I dunno how — "

"It's not the hard times I'm speakin' of now," said Ellen; "they're bad enough, goodness knows; but it's the bother we have all the time, and we can't tell how or why. Half the time the cow gives no milk, and when she does, you can make no butther wid it. The pig, the crathur, won't get fat; he ates everything he can reach, and still he looks like a basket wid a skin over it. The smoke of the fire comes down the chimney, the dishes are thrown on the floor, wid nobody near them, and such noises are goin' on all night long that never a wink of sleep can a body get. What we'll do at all if it goes on, I dunno."

"By all the books that ever was opened and shut," Peter added, "it's all thrue what she says, and more. What wid all that and what wid the throubles that's on the whole counthry, if I only had the money saved to do it, I'ld lave it all to-morrow and go to the States — I would so."

"Leave off the things you do that make you all these troubles," said the older Mrs. O'Brien, "and you'll have no more need to go to the States than others."

"What things are them that we do?" Ellen asked.

"Haven't I told you before this," said Mrs. O'Brien, "that it's the Good People that trouble you? If you'ld treat them well, as we do, they'ld never bother you. If you'ld even take good care never to harm them, it's likely they'ld never come near you."

"It's the fairies you're speakin' of," said Peter. "Sure I don't believe in them at all. It's old woman's nonsense that your head's full of, savin' your presence, Mrs. O'Brien. There's no fairies at all. Don't talk to me."

"You'ld better be more respectful to them, Peter," Mrs. O'Brien answered. "Say less about not believing in them and don't call them by that name, that they don't like. Call them 'the Good People' or 'the gentry.' They don't like the name that you called them, any more than they like those who disbelieve in them or those who try to know too much about them. Speak well about them and treat them well, as we do, and they'll not trouble you; maybe they'll even help you. Didn't you see, as you came in, how we left something for them to eat and drink outside the door there? We've not much, but they like fresh milk and clean water, and we always give them these, and they hold nothing but friendliness for us. Look and see now if they've taken what we left there for them after supper."

Peter went to the door and looked. "There's nothing in the dishes there," he said; "but how do we know it wasn't the pig that ate it, or some poor dog, maybe?"

"You don't know," said Mrs. O'Brien, "only as I tell you, and you'ld better be attending to them that know more than yourself. If you did chance to give a meal to some poor dog, instead of to the Good People, there'ld be no great harm done, but it's the Good People that get what we put there. We always leave it for them and they always come and take it, and it's that makes them friendly, and so they would be to you, if you did the same. But you do nothing for them, because you say you don't believe in them, and you do worse than nothing. Didn't I see Ellen the other evening throwing out some dirty water and never saying 'Take care of the water?'"

"And what if I did?" said Ellen. "Can't I throw out wather when I plase, widout talkin' about it?"

"You can if you like," said the old woman, "but when you throw out water without warning, it's as likely as not some of the Good People may be passing, and they don't like dirty water to be thrown on them; and so after that your cow gives no milk, your pig is thin, and your dishes are thrown around the room. Do as you like with your water, or with anything else, but if you anger the Good People, be sure they'll do you harm."

"It's superstitious you are. Mrs. O'Brien," said Peter; "I dunno what it is that's throubling us, but there's no fairies at all."

"Superstitious, is it?" said the old woman. "And so you're not superstitious at all, and you don't believe in the Good People! Now tell me, Peter Sullivan, when you came to that door just now and said 'God save all here,' like a decent man, why did you acd 'except the cat?' What did you mean by those words 'except the cat?' Tell me that now."

"Why, sure, Mrs. O'Brien," Peter answered, just a bit confused, "sure, we're told that cats is avil spirits, so we mustn't put blessings on them, and when we say 'God save all here,' we add onto it 'except the cat,' so as not to be calling down a blessing on an avil spirit."

"Ah!" said Mrs. O'Brien, "it's not the likes of you that's superstitious. You can't put a blessing on the poor cat, when you're blessing everybody and everything else in the house, for fear you'ld be putting it on an evil spirit; but you're not superstitions, and so you throw dirty water on the Good People as they're passing, and you call them by names that they don't like, and then you wonder what it is that's troubling you."

"No, Mrs. O'Brien,' said Peter, again, "I dunno what it is at all. It may be the avil spirits themselves, for what I know, and whatever it is. I'ld go away and leave it and leave the country, if I had the money to get to the States. I heard once of a man that was druv out of the counthry by a monsther that I suppose was maybe something like the fairies — like them in making trouble for the man, anyway. It was a great conger that lived in a hole in the Sligo River, and I suppose he was ten yards long, and the man was a diver. He was gettin' stones out of the bottom of the river, and the conger says to him, 'What are you afther there?' says he. 'Stones, sor,' says the diver. 'Hadn't you betther be goin?' says the conger. 'I think so, sor,' says the diver, and afther that he never stopped goin' till he got to the States."

"That's you, Peter," said the old woman; "you don't believe in the Good People or strange monsters or anything of the sort, but you want to run away from them."

If Peter had been quite honest about it, he could scarcely have said, even to himself, whether he believed that there were any fairies or not; but he was really afraid of them, though he put on such a bold front and said that he did not believe in them, to make people think that he was uncommonly knowing. "Mrs. O'Brien," he said, "do you think it's true, what they say, that in the States you can pick up goold everywhere in the streets?"

"What good would it do you if it was true?" she asked.

"What good would it do me? Are ye askin' what good would goold do me? Sure, then, wouldn't I pick up all of it I could carry, and wouldn't I take land wid it and pay rent and buy stock for a big farm and grow as rich as Damer? What good would goold be? Ha! Ha! What couldn't you do in a country where ye could be pickin' up goold in the street?"

"There's no gold to be picked up in the streets there, any more than here," said the old woman, "and if there was, it would be no use to you. Only suppose, now, that you had picked up all the gold you could carry, and that you wanted to buy a loaf of bread with it. And suppose you went into a baker's shop and chose even the smallest loaf of bread you could find, and threw down a whole gold sovereign for it — aye, or a hundred gold sovereigns. Would the baker sell you the bread for your gold, do you think? Wouldn't he say to you: 'Go on out of this, for the silly Irishman that you are! What for would I be giving you good bread for that gold of yours, when I can pick up as much and as good as that any minute here before my own door and keep my bread as well?' If you could find gold in the street, it would be worth no more than the stones that you find there."

"I don't know how that is, Mrs. O'Brien," said Peter, "but I can't see why goold wouldn't be goold, wherever you could find it."

"It's not sensible," said John, "to be talkin' of findin' gold in the streets, but there's a deal in what Peter says, for all that, and it's often I've thought, too, that I'ld go to the States and be away from all these throubles, if only we could save up the money to take us all there. It's not any gold or any riches I'm thinkin' about, but what I want to know, mother, is this: Could a man in the States, if he was strong and if he worked hard — and if he didn't drink a great deal — could he make enough to keep himself and his wife both, so that she needn't work too hard — not so that she would sit idle, I don't mean, but so that she needn't be doin' hard work and doin' it all the time — could he do that?"

"That's the sensible and the honest talk," said his mother; 'he could do that. Those that do nothing get nothing, in the States the same as anywhere else. But I've talked with them that know, and they tell me that in the States those that will work are paid for their work, and those that are strong and industrious and honest can keep their families from want, and that's more than some can do here, God help them!"

"It would be a great thing," said John, speaking slowly, as if he were trying to make himself believe this dream of a land where a man's work could make his wife and his children sure of a home and food — "a great thing. And do you think, mother — but no, no — I suppose not — do you think, if we was once there — do you think that I could work enough to make it so that it would be easier for you and for Kitty both? Could one do enough for three?"

"It would be easier than here, maybe," was all that the old woman said in answer to this. She had heard this talk of America many times before, and she did not like it. She would rather believe, and make others believe, that better times were coming for Ireland. She was not so young as the others and not so ready to leave her old home, yet lately she had seen how it was growing harder and harder to stay, and there seemed to be little left of the good luck of which she boasted.

She was thinking of all this now, and John knew her thoughts, though she did not speak them, and he said: "You always tell us that there's betther times comin', mother, and I've learned to know that all you say is true. She was sayin' it just before you came in, Pether. But how can we believe in the betther times? They don't come. They get worse and worse. How do we know they'll ever come?"

Again Mrs. O'Brien seemed lost in deep thought, or in a dream, just as when, a little while before, she had told them of O'Donoghue. What she told them now was a sort of answer to John's question, but perhaps she told it quite as much to draw their thoughts away from America. She was silent for a little while, and they all waited for her to speak.

"Good times for Ireland there will be again," she said, "when Earl Gerald comes back. It was hundreds of years ago that Earl Gerald lived in his great castle of Mullaghmast. He was a strong warrior and he fought many a good fight for his people against their foes. More than that, he was powerful in magic. He could work mighty charms and he could change himself into any form he liked.

"His wife knew that he could do this, but he had never shown himself to her in any form but his own. She often begged him to let her see what his magic could do, and to change himself to some other form for her. But he knew there was danger in it, and he put her off with one reason and another. But at last, she asked him so many times, he told her that if she took any fright at all while he was in any form but his own he could never live in the world again in his own form till all the people of the country had passed away many times. 'I'ld not be a fit wife for you,' she said, 'if I'ld be easily frightened.'

"'You might not be easily frightened,' he said, 'but you might have great cause, and if you were only a little frightened you would never see me like myself again.'

"Then one day, as they were sitting together, the Earl turned away his head and muttered some words which his wife could not understand, and that instant he was gone, and instead of him sitting beside her she saw a little goldfinch flying around the room. The goldfinch flew out at the window into the garden; then it flew back and sat on the lady's shoulder and on her hand and on her head, and it sang to her, and so they played together for a time. Then it flew out into the open air once more, but in a second it darted back through the window and straight into the lady's bosom. The next instant she saw a wild hawk, that was chasing the little bird and was coming straight through the window after it. She put both her hands over her bosom, to save her husband's life, but she was frightened and she gave one scream as the hawk darted into the room, dashed itself against a table, and was killed. Then she looked where the little bird had been, and it was gone. She never saw Earl Gerald again.

"But Earl Gerald was not dead, and he is not dead, though all this was hundreds of years ago. He is sleeping, down under the ground, just beneath where his old castle used to stand. His warriors are there with him. They are in a great hall. The Earl sits at the head of a long table and the men sit down the sides. All rest their heads upon the table and all are asleep. Against the wall there are rows of stalls, and behind each man, in one of the stalls, is his horse.

"Once in every seven years Earl Gerald wakes at night. He rises and mounts his horse. A door of the hall opens. He rides out into the free air. He rides around the Curragh of Kildare and then back into the cave, to sleep again for seven years.

"While he is out the door is open. Once, long ago, a horse-dealer was going home late, and he had been drinking a little. He saw the door in the hill open and he walked in. And there he found himself in a hall, dim and high. A row of dim lamps hung along the hall, and he saw the smoke of them rise up to the roof, where many old banners, faded and torn, stirred a little in the light breeze that came in by the open door. And the light of the lamps shone down and glistened on the bright armor of rows of men who sat with their steel helmets bowed upon the table, and behind them were rows of horses, with their saddles and their bridles on, ready for their riders.

"There was no sound in the cave but the shuffle of his own foot, and the stillness and the sight that he saw made him afraid. His hand trembled, and a bridle that he had fell upon the floor. The noise echoed and echoed through the cave, and the warrior who sat nearest to the poor man raised his head. 'Is it time?' the warrior said.

"'Not yet, but soon will be,' the man answered, and the warrior's head sank again upon the table. The man went out of the cave as quickly as he could, and he never could find the door of it again.

"They say that Earl Gerald's horse has silver shoes. They were half an inch thick when the Earl's sleep began. When they are worn as thin as a cat's ear it will be time. Then a miller's son, who will have six fingers on each hand, will blow a trumpet, and Earl Gerald and all his warriors will come out of the cave. They will fight a great battle and will conquer the enemies of Ireland. Then the country will be peaceful and prosperous and happy, and Gerald will be its King for forty years."

Peter's mind could not be set at rest by any such stories as this to-night. "What's the good of all thim old tales to us?" he asked, "Can we pay our rint wid the knowledge that Earl Gerald will be King of Ireland for forty years? They do be all the time fortellin' and prophesyin' and predictin' this thing and that thing and the other thing in thim old tales, and nothin' ever comes o' thim. Did you ever know, now, Mrs. O'Brien — I ask you — will you tell me this — did ye ever know of any of the prophecies in any of thim old woman's tales comin' thrue?"

"It's surprised I am," said the old woman, "to hear you, Peter Sullivan, talking that way — you, that had a decent man for your father, and that's a decent man yourself, all but knowing nothing — you, that have heard the stories of your people. Tell me now, did you ever hear what was foretold of the children of Lir, and did you ever hear if it came true or not?"

Perhaps Peter had never heard about the children of Lir, or perhaps he had heard and did not like to say so, because the story would be proof that a prophecy had come true. At any rate, he said nothing. But the old woman seemed resolved that if he had never heard about the children of Lir he should hear about them now.

"Lir was a powerful man in the old days of Ireland," she said, "He had three sons and one daughter, and their mother was dead. The names of the sons were Hugh, Fiachra, and Conn, and the name of the daughter was Fair-shoulder, and beautiful and good children were they all. Lir was visiting once at the castle of Bogha Derg, the King of Conacht, and he saw the daughter of the King, and he fell in love with her and married her.

"For a time they were happy, and then the new wife began to be jealous of the love of her husband for his four children. It troubled her so much that she began to lose her beauty and her health, and at last she took to her bed and did not leave it for a year. And after that time there came a great Druid to visit her. You know who and what the Druids were, I think. They were the priests of the old religion of Ireland, before St. Patrick came and made the people Christians. They were powerful in magic; they could bring storms and could drive them away; they could foretell the future; they could work powerful enchantments on people and beasts, and trees and stones, and they could do many other marvellous things.

"This Druid talked with the wife of Lir for a long time alone. He made her tell him all that troubled her, and then he told her what she could do to be rid of her husband's children. He gave her a magic wand and went on his way.

"Then she rose from her bed and took the four children with her in her chariot and set out for her father's castle. On the way she ordered the driver of the chariot to kill the children, but he refused. Then they passed near a lake, and the step-mother told the children to go into the water and bathe. But Fair-shoulder believed that she meant them some harm, and she refused to go, and begged her brothers not to go. So the step-mother called her men, and she and they forced the children out of the chariot and pushed them into the water. Then she touched each of them on the head with the Druid's wand, and they were changed into four beautiful white swans.

"After she had done that, she went on to her father's castle. When her father had welcomed her, he said, 'Where are your husband's children?'

"'They are at home,' she answered, 'in their father's castle.'

"'And are they well?'

"'They are well.'

"Now the King himself was a Druid, and more powerful than the one who had given his daughter the wand. More than that, he was a good man, and the other was a wicked one. He did not believe what his daughter told him about the children, and so he put her into a magic sleep. When she was asleep he said to her, 'Where are your husband's children?'

"And she answered, 'They are in the lake which we passed by the way as we came here.'

"'And what did you do to them?'

"'I changed them into white swans.'

"'Why did you do that?'

"'Because my husband loved them more than he loved me.'

"He woke her out of the magic sleep and called all his people together. Before them all he told her that she should be punished for her wickedness, and then he changed her, by his Druidic power, into a gray vulture. Then he said to the people: 'This creature that was my daughter has laid a wicked enchantment on her husband's children. She has changed them into swans. They must keep that shape for many hundreds of years; they must swim in the lakes and the seas and fly over the land, and they must travel far and must suffer much. But there is a hope for them. Many, many hundred years will pass away — so many that even the Druid's eye can scarcely see what is at the end of them. But at last

there shall come strange men across the sea to Erin — men with
shaven heads. They shall build houses and shall set up tables in
the east ends of their houses, and they shall ring bells. And when
the swans that were the children of Lir shall hear the first sound
of these bells, they shall have their human shape again, and then
they shall be happy forever. But she — the gray vulture — she
shall fly in the sky, where it is stormy and cold. Where there are
thick clouds and where the rain is made, there shall be her home.
She shall not fly where the heaven is blue and where the sun
shines warm. The bells of the good men from over the sea shall
bring her no peace. Her way shall be with the wind and the hail.
If she has any rest it shall be on the peak of some wet crag, where
the snow whirls around her, or the fog drives past her, or the sleet
cuts against her, or the cold spray of the sea dashes over her. And
it shall be so with her till the Day of Doom.'

"When the King had finished speaking the gray vulture flew
away, and she was never seen again. But the King and all the
court rode in chariots to the lake where the white swans were,
and Lir and all his people came there, too, when they heard what
had been done. And there they all stood and listened to the singing of the four swans. So beautiful was the song that those who
listened could think of nothing else while they heard it. They left
their horses and their chariots and stood on the shore of the lake
and listened to the enchanting music, and never thought of food,
or of drink, or of sleep. Even the horses listened to the song as the
people did. Day and night they stood there, and many days and
nights, and no hunger came upon them, and they felt no cold and
no heat, and no wind and no wet.

"But the time came when the enchantment that was upon
them compelled the four white swans to leave the place. They
rose up into the air and flew away and out of sight into the sky.
Then the King and his people, and Lir and his people, went back
to their castles, and they never saw the four white swans again.

"The four white swans flew to Loch Derg, and there for
many years they swam on the lake, and fed and slept among the
rushes along the shores. In the summer the lake was pleasant and
cool, the air was clear and mild, the sky was blue, and the sun

was bright and beautiful. Then Fair-shoulder and her brothers forgot that they were unhappy. They sang songs to one another and scarcely remembered that they had ever been anything but swans, swimming on this peaceful water. But when the winter came and the ice was all around, and the wind from the north blew the snow against them, so that it froze among their feathers and they could scarcely move, they were so stiff and so cold — then they remembered how happy they had been in their father's castle. They could not sing now — not even sad songs. They only longed to have their human shape again and to be back in their old home.

"But after many, many years more had passed they ceased to wish for home. They had been swans so long now that it did not seem to them that they had ever been anything else. When the winter came again and again and again, and the days of chilling storm and the nights of freezing darkness were upon them, the poor brothers longed for nothing but the end of it all. The thought of the old castle hall, with its bright fires and its feasts and its music of minstrels and its dances and its games, was only another pain to them, and they wished only to die and to leave their sorrows.

"Then they crowded close together, to be as warm as they could, and Fair-shoulder tried to spread her wings over her brothers, to keep the storm from them. She tried to comfort them, and she told them again and again the story that she had heard from the people who stood by the lake to hear them sing, the story that the King had told, that, after many hundreds of years, strange men should come across the sea to Erin — men with shaven heads; that they should build houses and set up tables in the east ends of their houses, and that they should ring bells; and when the swans should hear the first sound of those bells they should have their human shape again, and then they should be happy forever.

"For three hundred years they were at Loch Derg, and then, by the power of their enchantment, they were compelled to leave it. They flew to the sea of Moyle, and there they stayed, through the summer's heat and the winter's cold, for three hundred years more. Still the sister told her brothers of the strange men who were to come to Erin and of the bells that were to free them. But they could not be comforted. The strange men were too long in coming.

"When the three hundred years were past they had to fly away again to another sea. As they flew, they passed over the spot where their father's castle had stood and where they had been happy children together. Not a stone of the beautiful castle could they see. It had all crumbled down, and the grass had grown over it for many a year. They saw the fox that had its hole where their father's bright hearth fire had been, and they saw the ditch of dirty water where their father used to welcome kings and bards and wise men at his gate. They kept their way through the air and saw no more; yet they had seen all that there was to see. It gave the poor swans only a little ache at the heart, for they were past hope now. They had suffered too much to believe anything or to think of anything but the suffering that was past and the more suffering that was to come.

"The end of their journey came and they swam in a new sea. Again the sister tried to cheer her brothers, but they could not be cheered. The strange men with the shaven heads would never come, they thought. They had waited for them too long.

"But the hundreds of years that had passed had done more than to bring sorrow to the poor swans. In lands far away a new faith had grown up, not like the Druids' faith. And at last across the sea to Erin came the holy St. Patrick. He brought monks with him, and they had shaven heads. They went about the island and preached, and built chapels. In the east end of each chapel they set up an altar, and they said masses and rang bells. And they built a chapel on the island that has since been called the Isle of Glory.

"And so, one bright morning, Fair-shoulder and her brothers were swimming near the Isle of Glory, when, of a sudden, there came to them from the shore the sweet sound of a bell. Then Fair-shoulder called to her brothers, and they all swam to the shore. And as soon as they were on shore their form of swans was gone.

Fair-shoulder was a beautiful young girl again, and the brothers were strong, beautiful boys. They walked up to the little chapel together, and there a monk baptized them.

"And as soon as they were baptized they were young and strong no longer. Fair-shoulder was an old, old woman, and her brothers were old, old men. They were so weak with the age of a thousand years that they fell upon the floor of the chapel. The monks took them up and cared for them for a few days, and then they died. And so the word of the Druid came to pass, that when the strange men should ring their bells the children of Lir should be swans no longer, and should be happy forever."

They all waited for a few minutes, to be sure that there was no more of the story, and then John said: "Mother, it's easy for you to be tellin' us them tales, and they may be all thrue enough, and I'm not sayin' they're not. But what good are they to us? The word of the Druid came thrue, but how long was it in comin' thrue? A thousand years?"

"A thousand years or more," said his mother; "but the stories can teach us to be patient, if they can do nothing else."

"They may do that," said John; "the blessed Lord He knows you've been patient, and He knows the rest of us have tried to be. But what does it all come to? We can't wait a thousand years for the betther times. Pether, here, is right. The States would be a betther place for all of us. If we had the money I'ld say that we ought to go there."

"It's not the bad times alone that's in it," said Peter. "As I told you before, I could stand them. It's the bother that we're put to all the time. It's that would make us go to the States this minute, if we had the chance. But I suppose your mother could never be leavin' Ireland now, John; she's gettin' so old now, maybe she couldn't stand the journey."

"Have no fear about that," John answered; "mother's not so old as you'ld make out, and she's likely to live longer now than some others that's here this minute."

As he said this John felt Kitty's hand suddenly holding his closer, and he knew that he ought not to have said it. "Don't mind what I'm sayin'," he said to her in a whisper; "I dunno what I'm talkin' about, but I didn't mean you at all, darlin', nor anybody particular. It'll all come right somehow, and we'll soon see the roses back in your cheek, and the smile on your lips, and the light in your eyes. Don't mind what I said."

"But what's the use talkin' of it at all?" said Peter. "You've no money and we've less. We might as well be talkin' of goin' to the moon as to the States."

The old woman did not seem to be paying any attention to what the others were saying, and now nobody at all said any-thing for a little while. Then Mrs. O'Brien began: "John and Kitty, I think sometimes it's true I'm getting old and foolish. I don't know what has made me talk the way I have to-night I've seen it coming — oh, I've seen it coming all along — yes, longer than any one of you has seen it — and I knew I couldn't stand in the way. And yet to be leaving the old places — the old fields and hills and paths — the old streams and trees and rocks — the old places where your father and I walked and sat and talked so often to-gether, where you were born and where he lies — I couldn't bear to think of it. It's old and weak and foolish I'm getting, and I couldn't bear to think of it. And so I've tried to make you think of other things and to make you think that it would be better some-how, some time. Maybe I've said too much, and maybe I've kept you from going when you ought to have gone, but you'll know that it was because I couldn't bear to think of leaving all the dear places, and you'll forgive me; John and Kitty, you'll forgive me. I can say no more. If I couldn't think of it, yet I must do it. It is right that we should go, and we will go."

"And why should you be talkin that way, mother?" said John. "Was it what you said that kept us from goin' to the States long ago? Sure, if you had said nothing at all, we hadn't the money to go, and so what difference was it what you said?"

"Listen to me, John," said his mother; "it was all through me that you didn't leave this land of sorrow long ago. It was because it had been a land of joy as well to me that we all stayed here; and now, since you're sure that it's right and best for you to go, it's not the want of money that shall stand in your way. It's yourself knows, John, that your father — Heaven be his bed! — was always the careful and the saving man, and I always tried to help him the best I could. The times got a little better with us, as you know, after those worst ones in '47 and '48, and we saved a little again — it was not much, but it was something. Your father left it with me before he died, and he said: 'Keep it always by you till you need it most. Don't use it till the time comes when you can say, "I shall never need this money more than I need it now."' So I have always kept it, and I have it now. That was why I told you not to fear about the winter. It would have paid our rent if all else had failed, and it would have taken us all through the winter. But it's better that it should take us to the States. If we stayed here and used the money, we'ld be as bad off in another year. Kitty will be getting strong again there, and it'll be better for all of us. The time that your father said has come; I'm sure we'll never be needing the money that he left more than we're needing it now. There's no more to be said; we'll go."

For a little while no more was said. John and Kitty gazed at the old woman in wonder. The thing that they had thought about for so long, and wished for as a happiness that could never be, was come to them. And now it scarcely seemed a happiness; it was half a sorrow. Then Ellen spoke: "Oh, Mrs. O'Brien, it was always you was the good neighbor to us! It was always you was with us in joy and in sorrow! What'll we ever do at all when you're gone and we're left here alone, with none to be so kind to us as you've always been?"

And Peter said: "I was thinkin' that same. The Lord go wid you and keep you, wherever you go, but it'll be the sad day for us when you go away."

"Peter and Ellen," said the old woman "how could you think that we'ld do a thing like that? You may be a fool sometimes, Peter, but you're your father's son. Do you know what your father did for us, Peter? When my John was dying with the fever, he sat and watched with him, and brought him the water and the whey all night, and night after night, when I was so worn out that I could watch no longer. He might have taken the fever himself, and he might have died with it, and he did take it, but the Lord spared his life for a while after that, Heaven rest his soul! And another thing that John said to me before he died was this: 'As long as you have a bit to eat or a drop to drink or a penny to buy, never let Tom Sullivan or any of his want more than you want yourself.'

"And so, Peter and Ellen, when we go to the States, you'll both go too. There's enough of the money to take us all there. If you're ever able to pay it back, you can do it, if you like; but if not, we'll never ask you for it. If we went away from here without you, my husband would look down from Heaven and see me doing what he told me, with his dying breath, never to do. He would come to me at night and he would say: 'Mary, you are deserting in their sorrow the children of them that never deserted us in our sorrow.' Do you think that I could bear that? Do you think that I would do that?"

*****

Now I have told you all the talk that went on in the O'Briens' house that night. Perhaps you think that I have been a good while in doing it. If you will forgive me, I will try to get on with the story a little faster after this. Only one word more about this talk: you must not think that this was the first time that these five people had ever gone over and over this subject of America, or "the States," as they called it. They had talked of it many times, but Mrs. O'Brien had never given the word that they should go. The rest of them talked on and on of what they wished. But when she spoke, they all knew that she spoke of what was to be. They knew now that they should never talk of going again, but they should go.

III.
THE LITTLE GOOD PEOPLE

There was a good deal of commotion that night in the rath near where the O'Briens and the Sullivans lived. Do you know what a rath is? I suppose not. It is hard work to tell stories to you, you are so ignorant. I will tell you what a rath is. First I will tell you what it looks like. It looks like a mound of earth, in the shape of a ring, covered with turf, and perhaps with bushes. They are found all over Ireland. Some people, who have studied so much that they have lost all track of what they know and of what they don't know, say that these raths were made by the people who lived in Ireland many hundreds of years ago, and that they were strongholds to guard themselves and their sheep and their cattle from their enemies or from wild beasts. But people who know as much as Mrs. O'Brien, know that they are the places where the fairies live, or the Good People, as she would call them.

On this night that I have been telling you about, the Good People inside the rath were eating and drinking and dancing and making merry generally, as they do, you know, the most of the time. Perhaps you would like to have me tell you how the inside of the rath looked too. I will do the best I can. In the first place, the walls were all of silver and the floor was all of gold. Perhaps you don't know — no, I suppose you don't know — still you may happen to have heard of this before: the fairies know just where to find pretty much all the gold and silver and precious stones that there are in the world, if they happen to want them. They don't want much of them, of course — only just enough to make the walls and the roofs and the floors of their houses of, and to put all over their clothes and to make all their furniture and dishes of, and all their carriages and their boats, and a few other things — but they know where to find plenty of gold and silver, if they want it.

Now I think that I had better give you a little science. I believe that a book which children are to read, always ought to teach something, so I mean to teach you as much as I can. You must know, then, that gold is one of the heaviest things in the world. Now you know that the earth is always whirling round and round, so that the things that it is made of naturally get shaken up more or less. Besides that, it was once a good deal softer than it is now, so that the things that it is made of could move about more than they can now. And so the most of the gold, being, as I said, one of the heaviest things, got sifted down toward the bottom — that is, toward the centre of the earth. Only a little of it was left near the top, compared with what went to the bottom. It would not be at all surprising if the middle of the earth were a solid lump of gold, a thousand miles thick. But we poor men cannot dig down very deep into the earth. We can only scratch a little dirt off the top, and if we happen to grub up a few pounds of gold we think that we are rich, and the rest of the world thinks so too.

But the fairies laugh at us. They know how to go as deep into the earth as they choose, and so any fairy who chooses can give away gold all his life, and still have more of it in his dust-bin all the time than all the kings in the world have in their treasuries. And the other fairies don't call him rich.

But now we will go back to the rath. Of course it was all under the ground, so that there was no daylight. At the time we are talking about, there would not have been any anyway, for it was night. The place was lighted up with thousands of diamonds and rubies and emeralds, which were set all over the ceiling and shone like lamps. Now I won't call you ignorant just because you say that you don't understand how diamonds could light up anything, for I don't understand it myself. Let us talk about it together and try to decide. Suppose you try the experiment. Some night, after dark, take all the diamonds you have — every one of them — and carry them into a dark room and spread them out, and see if they light up the room at all. I am sure that you will find that they do not. On the contrary, if you let go of them, you will have to go and get a light to hunt for them by. But I suppose the fairies have some other kind of diamonds than ours, or else they know some other way of using the same kind. Sometimes they use fireflies, caught in spider-web nets, but these are generally for out of doors. To light up their houses they almost always use diamonds.

There were two tiny bits of turf fire in the rath. One of them was at one end of the hall, where the King sat, for the King to light his pipe by, and the other was at the other end, for the other fairy men to light their pipes by. Fairies do not like fire, as a rule, and they would never have any more of it about than they could help. But I know that they must have had some, for I know that Irish fairies smoke pipes, and how could they light them unless they kept a little fire on hand?

Now, I know what you will say to that. You will say: "If they could light a room with diamonds, why couldn't they light pipes with them?" Well, that is not very easy to answer, but I feel sure that even a fairy would never think of lighting a pipe with a diamond. I have owned up already that I don't know exactly how they light rooms with them, but it is easier for me to imagine a diamond giving light than giving heat. Isn't it for you? Now, be honest about it.

At one end of the hall sat the King and the Queen, on their thrones. Near them were half a dozen fairy men who were playing on pipes and fiddles. All over the floor there were dozens and scores of fairies, men and women, dancing to the music. All around the walls stood or sat many more of them, looking at the dancers, and now and then applauding and shouting at particular ones, or talking together, or simply smoking their pipes.

Suddenly two fairies rushed into the hall, with a little sound like the noise of a humming-bird's wings when it passes close to you. From the lower end of the hall, where they came in, they went straight through the crowd to where the King and Queen sat. They dropped on their knees before them for an instant, and then rose and spoke to them. In a moment the King clapped his hands, with a sign for the pipers and the fiddlers to stop playing. The instant that they stopped, everybody in the hall was still.

The King stood up and said to them: "Will ye be still now and listen, all of ye, to the news that's come to me this minute, and then will ye help me to think what we're to do about it at all?

Here's these two that's just come in, and they're just afther tellin' me that they've been at the O'Briens' house this evenin', and there they heard talk betune the O'Briens and the Sullivans, and it's all decided that both the O'Briens and the Sullivans is goin' to the States. And it's sorry I'll be to see the O'Briens lavin' the counthry. I don't care so much for the Sullivans."

"It was the O'Briens," said the Queen, "that always put the bit and sup outside the door for us, and what we'll be doin' widout the milk and the pertaties and the fresh wather, I dunno."

"Ye needn't be throubled about that," the King answered; "haven't we always enough to eat and drink of our own, what-ever happens?"

"Thrue for you," said the Queen, "we have our own food and drink, but it's not the same that we get from human people. Ye know that same yourself, and it's you as much as any that'll be missin' them things when the O'Briens is gone."

"That's the thrue word too," said the King; "it'll be the bad day for us all out, when they go. What for are they lavin' the counthry at all?"

"If ye plase, Your Majesty," said one of the fairies who had brought the news, "we heard all that too. It's the hard times that's in it. It's that makes them all want to go, and then, more than that, it's the bother the Sullivans are put to all the time, wid the cow givin' no milk and the pig not gettin' fat, and all that, and they're bound that they'll go away and stand it no longer."

"Is that it?" said the King. "It's that divil Naggeneen that's in it. I told him he could bother them a little if he liked, but not to bother them too much, and now he's drivin' them and their neighbors out of the counthry, and we all have to suffer for it. He'll make it up to us in some way, if they go, or I'll take it out of him. Come here, Naggeneen! What are ye doin' down there by yourself? Come up here and stand forninst me, till I give ye a piece of me mind. Now, what's all this about the O'Briens and the Sullivans lavin' the counthry? What have ye been about wid them?"

A fairy who had not been in the hall before had just come in at the far end from the King, who had caught sight of him. He was smoking a pipe. He had his hands in the pockets of his little green breeches, he wore a red jacket, and on his head was a red cap. He came slowly up the hall, when the King called him, and stood before the throne. "Take off your cap, ye worthless vagabone," said the King, "when you speak to me."

"I wasn't spakin' to you," said Naggeneen; "it was you that spoke to me. You called me, and here I am to the fore, though I don't belong to your pitiful little thribe, and I needn't come when you call, if I don't like."

"Oh, needn't ye?" said the King. 'Take off your cap now, or it'll be taken off for ye."

Naggeneen took off his cap.

"Now," said the King, "what have ye been doin' to the Sullivans, that they're lavin' the counthry and persuadin' the O'Briens to go wid them?"

"I've been doin' nothin'," said Naggeneen, "but what you said I might do."

"Oh, haven't ye?" said the King. "And what was that?"

"Oh," said Naggeneen, "I just took all the cream and the most of the milk from their cow, and you yourself had a share of it, as you know well; and I put a charm on their pig, so that it wouldn't get fat, no matter how much it 'uld be atin'; and then I druv the smoke of their fire down the chimney, and I threw the dishes and the pans around in the night, just so they wouldn't get lazy wid restin' too well, and a few more little things like that."

"Was that all ye did?" said the King. "And how long have ye been at it that way?"

"Ever since the day that Mrs. Sullivan threw the dirthy wather on me, as I was passin' the house. But I'm not the only one that's in it. Some of your own people here have helped me, and good they are at divilment too."

"And those things was all you did, was they?" said the King. "And didn't I tell ye ye could bother them a little, but not too much? What would ye have done if I had told ye to do what ye liked wid them?"

"What would I have done then? Oh, I'ld have shown ye the real fun then. What would I have done then? I'ld have pinched them and stuck pins in them all day and all night. I'ld have put charms on themselves, so that they'ld grow thinner than the pig. I'ld have took the pertaties out of the creel when they were put to drain at the door. If they went away from home I'ld make them think that they saw their house burning up, and so I'ld scare them to death. What would I do if you gave me leave? What wouldn't I do?"

"Well, you've done enough as it is," said the King, "to get the whole of us into throuble, and now let's hear what you're goin' to do to get us out of it. Here they are lavin' the counthry and takin' the O'Briens wid them, that was always the good neighbors to us, and they themselves were sometimes useful in their own way, in spite of themselves. And now I ask ye, Naggeneen, what are ye goin' to do to get us out of the throuble ye've got us into?"

"I'm in no throuble meself," Naggeneen answered, "and I dunno what I have to do wid any throuble that you may be in."

"You're in no throuble yourself? Haven't ye been as good as livin' on the Sullivans all this time? And now what are ye goin' to do widout them?"

"I'm goin' to do nothin' widout them; I'm goin' wid them."

"Goin' wid them! Goin' wid them!"

"Them was me words; you and your silly little thribe can do what ye like; I'm goin' wid them. It's a stuffy little place, this rath of yours, and I've a notion thravellin' would be good for me health, any way."

"But how can ye go wid them?"

"It's not hard at all," said Naggeneen, "and it's been done before this. I was near doin' it meself once. I don't suppose ye remember me old friend MacCarthy."

"MacCarthy of Ballinacarthy?" the King asked.

"The same," said Naggeneen, "and it was he was the good friend to mortal or fairy. It was he kept the good house and the good table and the good cellar — more especially the good cellar. That was not so many years ago — a hundred and odd, maybe. A fine man he was; we don't see his like now. I lived wid him the most of the time — in the cellar. And the strange thing about him was that, though nobody ever had a bad word for him, though all his servants said that he was the kindest and the best masther that ever stepped, he could get nobody to stay in the place of butler. It was all well enough wid the rest — cooks, maids, hostlers, stable boys — but the first time ever a new butler went into that beautiful wine cellar for wine, back he'ld come in a hurry and say that he'ld lave his place the next day, and nothing on earth would keep him in it. Now, wasn't that strange?"

"Did you say you lived in that cellar?" the King asked.

"The most of the time," said Naggeneen.

"Then it was not strange," said the King.

"Any way, strange or not strange," Naggeneen went on. "it was the truth. Never a butler could he keep in his service. A new butler would come and he'ld think he was a made man, old MacCarthy was that well known and that well liked all over the counthry. He'ld wait once at dinner and then down he'ld go tc the cellar for wine. Sometimes he'ld come back wid the wine and oftener he'ld come back widout it, but every time he'ld say: Mr. MacCarthy, sir, it's much obliged to you I am for all your kindness, but I'll have to be lavin' your service to-morrow.' And nobody could see the why of it.

"And at long last there was young Jack Leary, that had been all his life in old MacCarthy's stable, and he knew how the old man was bad off for a butler, and he made bold to ask for the place. 'If I make ye me butler,' says the old man, 'will ye go into the cellar and bring the wine when I ask ye, and make no throuble about it?'

"'Is that all?' says Jack; 'sure, yer honor, I'ld be glad to spend all me time, day and night, in the cellar, only ye might be wantin' me somewhere else now and then.'

"'Then look sharp,' says old MacCarthy, 'for there's gintlemin comin' to dinner to-day. Wait on the table the best ye know how, and at the end of it, when I ring the bell three times, do ye go to the cellar and bring plenty of wine, and let's have no more nonsinse about it.'

"'Niver say it twice,' says Jack; 'yer honor can depind on me.'

"Well, ye may belave I was listenin' to all this, for I wasn't in the cellar all the time. 'His honor may say it twice,' says I to meself, 'or as many times as he likes, but you'll never go into that cellar twice, Jack, me fine boy.'

"So Jack went about his work, and the dinner went all well enough, till late in the evenin', when old MacCarthy rang the bell three times, and off started Jack for the cellar, wid a basket to bring back the wine. 'It's the silly lot they war,' says he to himself, 'thim butlers, that they'ld be afraid to go to the cellar and bring back a bit of a basket full of wine. The only thing I don't like about it is that I can't bring it back in me skin instead of in the basket.'

"He was thinkin' like this in his mind as he went down the long, dark stairs wid his candle, and you may depend I was ready for him, by the time he got to the bottom. So no sooner did he touch the key to the lock than I give him a sort of a laugh and a scream that set the empty wine bottles that stood outside the door a-dancin' together. Jack was a good bold boy, sure enough, and he got the key into the lock and turned it. Wid that I swung the door open for him, so hard that it crashed against the wall and near shook the house down. And then me fine boy saw all the casks and the hogsheads in the cellar a-swingin' and a-rockin' and a-whirlin' around, as if all the wine had been in him instead of in them.

"You may be sure he didn't wait long afther that, but he just dropped his basket and fell all the way up the stairs and into the room where the gintlemin was waitin' for their wine. Well, it was then that old MacCarthy was in the towerin' rage. Never a word could Jack say to tell where he'd been or how he came back, or why.

"'Gintlemin,' says MacCarthy, 'ye'll get your wine, if I have to go to the cellar for it meself. But this I tell ye: I'll live no longer in this house, where I can't get servants to serve me. I'll be lavin' it to-morrow, and no later. The next time ye find me at home, ye'll find me in a place where I can keep a butler and have him do his work.'

"Wid that he took the lantern and started for the cellar himself. Ye'll guess that I was in the dining-room as soon as Jack and heard all this, and I was back in the cellar, too, before MacCarthy got there. I was sittin' on a cask of port, when he came in and saw me be the light of the lantern. I was sittin' there, wid a spiggot over me shoulder. 'Are ye there?' says MacCarthy. 'Who are ye, anyway, and what are ye doin' there?'

"'Sure, your honor,' says I, 'a'n't we goin' to move to-morrow, and it's not the likes of a kind man like you that would be wishin' to lave poor little Naggeneen behind.'

"'Is that the way of it?' says MacCarthy. 'Well, if you're agoin' to move wid us, I see no use in movin' at all. If I'm to have you in me cellar, wherever it is, it may as well be at Ballinacarthy as anywhere.'

"And from that day till the day of his death me and old Mac-Carthy was the best of friends. And he always brought all his wine from the cellar himself."

"And what has all that to do wid us?" said the King.

"What has it to do wid ye?" said Naggeneen. "It has nothin' to do wid ye, unless ye want to make it, and never a care I care whether ye do or not. But it has a good deal to do wid me. It shows, doesn't it, that I was ready to go wid old MacCarthy, and him runnin' away from me; and just so I'm ready to go wid the Sullivans, now that they're runnin' away from me. I've given ye a good hint. Ye can do as ye plase."

"It's glad I'ld be," said the Queen, "if we could be rid of the Sullivans and Naggeneen both at once, but I dunno what we'll do at all if the O'Briens go away."

"I'm not over-fond of Naggeneen meself," said the King, "but it's a sharp bit of a boy he is, and I'm thinkin' he may not be far from right this time. It might be that a new counthry would be as good for us as for the O'Briens or the Sullivans, and, anyway, we'ld still be near to them."

"Do ye mean," the Queen said, "that ye think we might all go to the States along wid the O'Briens and the Sullivans and Naggeneen?"

"If Naggeneen goes," the King replied, "he'll go along wid us; we'll not go wid him; but it was just that same that I was thinkin'. And yet we couldn't do a thing like that widout the lave of me King of All Ireland."

When the King spoke of the King of All Ireland, of course he meant the King of all the fairies in Ireland. He was himself only the King of this rath. Of course you know that the people of Ireland have no kings of their own any more.

"Naggeneen, me boy," said the King, "just take your fut in your hand and go to the King of All Ireland. Give him me compliments and ask him would he think there was anything against the whole of us goin' to the States."

"Is it me that would be runnin' arrants to the King of All Ireland," Naggeneen answered: "me, that don't belong to your thribe at all, and forty lazy spalpeens around here wearin' their legs off wid dancin' or rustin' them off wid doin' nothin' at all?"

"It's thrue you don't belong to me thribe," said the King, "and glad I am of that same. But while ye stay in me rath ye'll do what I bid ye. Why would I kape a dog and bark meself? Go on, now, and do what I tell ye, or ye know what I'll do to ye. Be off now!'

Naggeneen was off.

Now, while Naggeneen is gone with his message to the King of All Ireland, I will just take a minute to say something that I have felt like saying for quite a little while. He will not be gone much more than a minute. What I have to say is this: Nearly all the people in this story, mortals and fairies, too, had the way of speaking that most Irish people have, which we call a brogue. Mrs. O'Brien had only a little of it — just the bit of a soft brogue that comes from Dublin, where she had lived for a long time. The most of the others had a good deal more. But as I go on with the story from here, I see no use in trying to write the brogue. It is hard to spell and confusing to read. If you do not know what a good Irish brogue is, you would never learn from any attempt of mine to spell it out for you; and if you do know what it is, you can put it in for yourself. I may have to try to write a little of it now and then, for there is some Irish that does not look like Irish when it is written in English, but I shall use as little of it after this as I can. Naggeneen is back by this time.

Naggeneen sauntered into the hall where the King and the Queen and all the company were waiting for him, with his hands in his pockets, quite as if he had been out for a quiet stroll and had come back because he was tired of it. "Well," said the King, "did you see the King of All Ireland?"

"I saw him with my good-looking eyes," Naggeneen answered.

"And what did he say?"

"He said he'ld come here and talk to you himself, and, by the look of him, I think it's a pleasant time he'll be giving you."

"Then why is he not here as soon as you?" the King asked.

"Oh, nothing would do for him," said Naggeneen, "but that he and his men must come on horseback. They can come no faster that way, but they think it's due to their dignity. They had to wait for the horses to be ready, and so I beat them."

Naggeneen had scarcely said this when the door flew open at the end of the hall, and, with a rush and a whirl, in came a great troupe of fairies on horseback — the King of All Ireland and his men. They all leaped down from their horses, and instantly every horse turned into a green rush, such as grows beside the bogs. The King of All Ireland walked quickly up to the King of the rath and stood before him, with an awful frown on his face. The King of the rath was plainly nervous. "Will you have a light for your pipe, Your Majesty?" he asked.

"Never mind my pipe now," said the King of All Ireland. "Tell me first of all, who is this messenger that you sent to me?" The King of All Ireland had only a little bit of brogue — the Dublin kind.

"Sure," said the King of the rath, "that's only poor Naggeneen."

"Only poor Naggeneen!" cried the King of All Ireland. "And what are you doing with him? Do you see the red jacket he has on? Why doesn't he wear a green jacket, like your people? You know what his red jacket means as well as I. He belongs to the fairies who live by themselves, not to those who live together honestly in a rath. Why do you have him with your honest green jackets?"

"Sure, Your Majesty," said the King of the rath, "I thought it was no harm. He said he was tired of being by himself, and you know how handy he is with the fiddle or the pipes. If he'd been a fir darrig, that's always playing tricks and making trouble everywhere, why, then, of course — but he was only a poor cluricaun — "

"Yes," the King of All Ireland interrupted, "only a poor cluricaun, that does nothing but rob gentlemen's wine cellars and keep himself so drunk that he's of no use when he's wanted for any good. And hasn't he made you as much trouble as any fir darrig could do?"

"I was a lepracaun, too, once, Your Majesty," Naggeneen said.

"A lepracaun, were you? What did you do then? And when was it and how did it happen that a lazy lump like you was ever a lepracaun?"

"It was a long time ago," said Naggeneen, ready enough to talk about anything to draw the King's thoughts away from the trouble that he had made. "After old MacCarthy, of Ballinacarthy, died, those that came after him did not keep up his cellar well, and I felt lonely and sad, and I didn't care to drink any more — "

"Lonely and sad you must have been," said the King of All Ireland; "but you did drink still, did you not, though you didn't care for it?"

"True for you, Your Majesty," said Naggeneen, "I did a little, just for my health. But I was so lonely and so falling to pieces with idleness — "

"Falling to pieces with idleness!" the King interrupted again. "If idleness could make you fall to pieces, there wouldn't have been a piece of you left big enough to make trouble in a fly's eye, these last seven hundred years."

"As you say, Your Majesty," Naggeneen went on, "but, any-way, I was a lepracaun, and I did what any other lepracaun does: I sat in the field or under a tree and made brogues. But it was sorry work and people was always trying to catch me, to make me show them the gold they thought I had. And one time a great brute of a spalpeen did catch me, and he nearly broke me in two with the squeeze he gave me, so that I wouldn't get away till I'd showed him the gold. And I nearly had to show it to him, but I made him look away for a second, and then of course I was off. And after that my friend the King here let me come and live in the rath, just for company — not that I belong to his little tribe at all."

"And now you see," said the King of All Ireland, turning from Naggeneen to the King of the rath, "what trouble comes to you from taking those into your rath that have no right there. He's sending people out of Ireland that might be of use to you and to all of us. He wants to go with them, and that is no loss, but you want to go, too and to take all your people. That might be a loss, though I don't know that it would."

"We think it's best that we should go, Your Majesty," the King of the rath answered, meekly, "if you see no reason why not."

"I see reasons enough why not," said the King of All Ireland. "You don't know where you are going, nor what you'll find there. You don't know how you're to live, nor whether it'll be any fit place to live. You don't know whether the people there will help you or hinder you."

"Wherever the O'Briens go, they'll help us," the King of the rath answered. "We don't like to have them leave us here."

"You've gone contrary to the law enough already," said the King of All Ireland, "in taking in this fellow with the red coat. Now you may take all the consequences of it and go where you like. I don't care where you go and I think nobody cares, only I think it may be best for all the Good People in Ireland to have you out of it. Mount your horses," he shouted to his men, "and we'll be off out of this!"

He took one of the little green rushes from the floor and sat astride it, as a little boy rides on his father's cane. "Borram, borram, borram!" he said, and instantly the rush was a beautiful white horse. Every one of his men did the same. Each one took one of the rushes and sat astride of it and said, "Borram, borram, borram!" and every one of the rushes grew into a horse. There was a little whirring sound, like that of a swarm of bees, and they were all gone.

Everybody in the rath was silent for a few minutes. The King and the Queen looked at each other and were much troubled. Naggeneen, without making a bit of noise, scuttled down to the farthest corner of the hall. The others seemed not to know where to look or what to do or to think. Then the King turned toward them and said; "It's all over; we couldn't stay here now. Wherever has Naggeneen got to?"

The fairies who were nearest to Naggeneen hustled him forward and he stood before the King again. "Naggeneen," said the King, "it's trouble enough you've made for all of us, and it's bellyragging enough you and all the rest of us have got for it, and we don't know, as His Majesty said, what more is to come. So now do the only thing you was ever good for and give us a tune out of the fiddle."

It was the only thing that Naggeneen was good for, and the only thing that was not mischief that he liked to do. He took a fiddle from one of the fairies who had been playing for the dancing before all the confusion began. He held the fiddle under his chin for a moment, while everybody waited, and then he began to play.

He played first some old tunes that every fairy in Ireland knows well. But not every fairy in Ireland can play them as Naggeneen did. They were tunes which everybody listening in that rath had known for hundreds of years. There were wild and strange airs that made them remember days when Ireland was a strange country, even to them; then the music was full of wonder and mystery, like the spells of the old Druids; then it was strong and free and fierce, and they thought of Finn McCool and the Fenians, and the days when Erin had heroes to guard her from her foes. The fiddle was telling them the story of their own lives and of all that they had ever seen and known. Now it was a strange music, which they could not understand — which the player could understand as little as the rest — but it was soft and sweet, and yet deep and bold, and the fairies trembled as they remembered the holy Patrick and a mighty power in the worlds of the seen and of the unseen. This passed away and the music came with the stir and the swing of marching men, and the fairies were again in the days of King Brian Boru, with Ireland free and brave and strong. It grew sad; it gushed out like sobs from a broken heart; then it was quieter, but still full of a softer sorrow; now it was merry and reckless. It made the fairies remember all that they had ever seen in the lives of the people whom they had known so long — the cruel hardship, war, sickness, hunger, and then, besides, the faith, the kindliness, the light-heartedness that had saved them through it all. There were tunes that every man and woman in Ireland knows — tunes that you know — old airs that every Irish fiddler or piper or singer learns from the older ones, that the oldest ones of all learned, they say, from the fairies. And under all the music, whether grave or gay, there went a strain of grief, sometimes almost harsh and sometimes scarcely heard, and as the fairies listened to it they grew pale at the thought that now they were to go away from all that they had known, to find something which they did not know. While they were thinking of this the music changed again. It was a soft murmur, like the sound of the sea that is kept forever in a sea-shell. Then it grew loud and rough, with the rush of winds and the crash of waves. The fairies were filled with fright, and before they knew that they were afraid, the music was singing a song of hope, and then, all at once, it grew as merry as if there had never been a sad thought in the world.

For a moment the fairies listened to it and all their feet began to stir restlessly on the floor. One of the fairy men caught the hand of a fairy girl — a fairy girl with cheeks like the tiny petals in the heart of a rose, with a white gown like a mist, and hair like fine sunbeams falling on the mist; he threw his arm about her waist, and they danced away down the hall. In an instant all the rest were dancing, too, alone, in pairs, and in rings. Naggeneen looked on and laughed till he could scarcely play. All this time his music had moved him less than anybody else who heard it. He did not feel what he had made the others feel, but he knew how to pour it all out of his fiddle.

The King made a sign for him to stop. All the dancers were still in an instant. The lights in the hall went out. The next minute, if you had been outside the rath and had laid your ear down on the turf which covered it, you would have heard nothing more than you might hear under the turf at any other time or in any other place.

IV.
THE CLEVERNESS OF MORTALS

If you live in the city of New York, or if you have ever been in the city of New York for any long time, you know how disheartening, how terrible, and how altogether unreasonable the climate can be at times. But you also know how heavenly it can be on an autumn day, when the sky and the air and the water are all in a good humor. To see and to feel the best of it, you must be down in the Narrows, or somewhere near there. The fierce heat has gone out of the air, but there is a gentle warmth left in it. All the shores near you are turning from green to brown and yellow, with here and there a dash of red. The sun makes every sail in the bay a gleaming spot of white. Far up the bay you see just an end of the city, with the tall buildings standing so close that it looks like one great castle, built all over a hill that slopes steeply down to the water on both sides. The Bridge looks like a spider's web, spun across to the other shore. Beyond it all the hills look purple, through the thin mist. If, instead of having seen all this often, you saw it for the first time — if you were coming from a far country, where you had always been poor — if you had toiled all your life to pay your rent, never expecting to do more — then perhaps you would look, more than anything else, at the giant woman standing before you and holding her torch high into the sky to light the world.

It was on such a day as this that the O'Briens and the Sullivans saw New York first. It was on the same day that the fairies who had left the rath and followed them saw it too. The O'Briens and the Sullivans had left their old home and gone to Queenstown, and the fairies had followed them. Cork and Queenstown had rather alarmed the fairies. They did not like the look of a city. It looked cold and stony and uncomfortable. It did not look like a good place to dance out of doors at night. They almost wished that they had stayed at home and let the O'Briens and the Sullivans go where they liked without them. Some of them even wanted to go back, but Naggeneen laughed at them, and fairies can stand being laughed at even less than human beings. But they all hoped that when the O'Briens and the Sullivans got wherever they were going, it would not prove to be in a city.

Then the O'Briens and the Sullivans went on board a ship and were stowed away in a place forward, with many other people, which the fairies did not think roomy or airy or pleasant in any way. But they were not obliged to stay in it. They found better places on the ship. Nobody could see them, so they went where they liked. They went out on the bow, where the lookout stood, and watched with him for sails and for tiny puffs of smoke by day and for little glimmers of light by night. They ran about the bridge and swarmed up the rigging. They even danced on the deck, as if they were in a field at home; and the deck was dewy at night, just like the field. They fluttered and whirled in circles around the red light on the one side of the ship and the green light on the other side, and they reminded them of the rubies and the emeralds that had helped to light their own rath.

One day they saw swimming in the water beside the ship an ugly creature, like a man, with a red nose, tangled green hair, green teeth, and fingers with webs between them, like a duck's foot. There was another creature, like a woman, very beautiful, but with green hair, like the man. These were merrows — sea fairies.

"Where are you bound in that ship?" the merrows called to them.

"WHERE ARE YOU BOUND IN THAT SHIP?"

"Where would we be bound at all," the King answered, "but to the States, where the ship's bound?"

"And what are ye goin' there for?" the merrows asked again.

"Sure," said Naggeneen, "it's followin' the O'Briens and the Sullivans we are, and it's the long way they're takin' us."

"Could you tell us what the States is like at all?" asked the King. "Is it like Cork?"

"There's parts of them," said the man merrow, "that's more like Cork than Cork itself, and there's other parts of them that's no more like Cork than the sea here is like Cork Harbor."

"But are there no places there," the King asked again, "like the country parts of Ireland, with the fields and the bogs and all?"

"I can't tell you that," the merrow answered. "We've never been far on the land. Deep down under the sea it's the same way it is under the sea about Ireland. There's the land at the bottom, with the sand all fine and firm, like a floor, and there's the water above, like a green sky, and there are the shells and the sea-flowers, and there are the weeds that wave around you and over you, like red and green and purple curtains to your house, and it's all as cool and as neat as any of the sea-places around Ireland. And if you like to go up to get the warmth of the sun or the light of the stars, there's white sand where you can lie at your ease, and there's great rocks where you can sit and look out over the sea and get the fresh breeze. And that's all we know of it; we've not been away from the sea."

And after a week of voyaging through the sea — after going on and on for so long and so far that both fairies and mortals began to think that they must soon fall over the edge of the earth — the ship suddenly stood up straight, instead of rolling and pitching about, and a little later they saw the giant woman before them, holding up her torch, and beyond her they saw the city. And then it was only a bit of a while longer till they came close to the city.

"Look at it!" cried the King to all the fairies, who were crowded at the bow; "it's like the country, after all! Look at all the grass and the trees! But it has an iron chain all around it. I don't like the look of that." All fairies hate iron. They more than hate it; they simply cannot endure it. To touch any iron at all would hurt

a fairy more than it would hurt you to touch it when it was red
hot.

"But it's only a small place, anyway," said Naggeneen. "Look
at the houses beyond there! There was nothing like them in Cork!
And do you mind them strings of coaches, running along up in
the air?"

"I was takin' note of them," said the King; "sure it's the
strange country!"

The fairies all followed the O'Briens and the Sullivans. They
were resolved not to lose sight of their only friends, in a land like
this. They found that the O'Briens and the Sullivans were quickly
taken to a big round house, in the very bit of a place like the
country that they had first seen. The fairies did not like the inside
of the big round house, so the King left a few to watch the
O'Briens and the Sullivans, and to bring word if they made any
important move, and the rest went out and found pleasanter
places on the grass and under the trees. They had managed to get
into the Battery Park without touching any of the horrible iron
chains that were around it. They would have been a very sorry-
looking company, if anybody could have seen them.

"I don't like it at all," the King said, "and nothing would
please me better than to be at home again. If they're going to live
in that big round house, I dunno what we'll do. We want to be
near to them, and yet this is no place for us. We could stand it a
little while, maybe. The grass is fine and smooth for dancing, but
these lights, like suns, that they have all around on the tops of the
poles, are terrible. Do they want no night at all here? And then
what a noise there is! It's nothing but rattle and roar all day, and
then the boats do be screeching around all night."

"Have no fear," said the Queen. 'The O'Briens would never
live in a place like this. They'll soon be out of it, and then we'll
follow them and find a better place near where they go."

It proved that the Queen was right. Before long there came
an alarm from those who had been left to watch, that the O'Briens
and the Sullivans were coming out. In a moment more they came,

and the whole tribe followed them. Old Mrs. O'Brien, who never forgot anything that was worth remembering, had not forgotten to write to some old friends who had come to America years before, that she and her son and his wife and their neighbors were coming. These old friends had found tenements for them, and soon they were in new homes. There was enough of Mrs. O'Brien's money to keep them for a little while, and they hoped that before it was gone, John and Peter would find work and would be getting more money.

The fairies followed them, filled with more and more wonder. For miles they followed, and then for more miles. It was not that the distance troubled them. They could have gone a hundred times as far without thinking of being tired. But they could scarcely believe their eyes when they saw these never-ending stone roads and these never-ending rows of stone and brick houses, all built so that they touched one another. They could not understand how people could live so close together, nor why they should want to do it, if they could. Perhaps you have never thought of it, but it is really true that the ways of mortals are just as wonderful to fairies as the ways of fairies are to mortals.

Indeed, the place where they found themselves at last was not a pleasant one for fairies. It was two places, in fact, but they were so much alike that there was nothing to choose between them. A tenement had been found for the O'Briens, up many flights of stairs, in a house with many other tenements. There was barely enough room in it for them to live, though it was better, in that respect, than their old cabin in Ireland. The stairs and the passage were far from clean, and they led down to a street that was just as far from clean.

It was hard all over with square stones, which had sunk, in places, and made hollows, which were filled with muddy water. Lean cats scuttled about here and there, and ran away, if anybody came near them, as if they expected to have stones thrown at them, and then, when the danger seemed past, they rummaged in the ash-barrels for scraps of meat or fish or bread. The people who lived in the houses sat on the doorsteps and on the curbstones, and chattered and laughed and quarrelled and slept. The sun shone into the street, but it could not shine between the houses. A breeze blew up from the East River, which was not far away, but the air was none too fresh, for all that. The place that had been found for the Sullivans was in another street, not far away. It was much the same, as I have said, but it was even smaller, for there were only two of the Sullivans, and they could get on with less space.

The fairies were fairly terrified at all this. And was it any wonder? The poor little Good People! They had been used to a beautiful, bright hall, to green, fresh grass to dance on in the quiet, misty moonlight, and to cool shade for the day. What could they do in such a place as this? They remembered how the King of All Ireland had told them that they did not know whether the place where they were going was a place fit for them to live in.

The first thing that the King did was to send some of the fairies in all directions to see if they could spy out any place where the whole tribe could live in a decent and comfortable manner. The street, he was sure, would never do. Of course, if the Fairy King wanted a rock or a hill to open and let him into it, it would open, and he could live in it, if he chose, just as he used to in his own old rath. And no mortal who might happen to be about would know that anything unusual was happening. And just so the street would open for him, if he wanted it to. But before he had decided to try it he saw a place where some men had opened it, and that was quite enough for him. If you have ever seen a New York street opened, you know what it was like; if you have not, it is of no use to try to tell you.

But the messengers whom the King had sent in all directions were scarcely gone when those who had started toward the west were back with joyful news. "We have found a beautiful place," they said. "It's only a bit of a way from here, and if we live there we'll not be far from the O'Briens. Ye never saw grass smoother in your life, though it's not quite so green, maybe, as it is at home. And then there's tall trees of all kinds, and there's bushes that'll have flowers on them, belike, in the right time of the year. And there's smooth roads and walks, and there's hills and great rocks, that we could live inside of as easy as in a rath itself. It's a much quieter place than here, too, and the air is better, though it's so near. It's not wide toward the west, but off to the south it reaches as far as we can see, like a forest."

The King left a guard to watch, lest the O'Briens should like the place as little as himself and should leave it and be lost, and then he hurried with the rest to see the new country that had been discovered. If you know New York very well indeed, you have guessed already that it was the north end of Central Park which the fairies had found. But you may know New York pretty well and not know, as a good many people who live in it do not, that there is any north end to Central Park, still less that it is far prettier than the south end.

After all the distressing streets and houses that he had seen, the King was delighted with it. He found a big rock, which was the base of a hill, and at the top of it stood a queer little square stone house. Back in this hill, he declared, behind the rock and under the stone house, would be as pleasant a place to live as ever the rath was. He made the rock open, and he and all the fairies with him went in, although the policemen and the men and women in carriages and on horses and on bicycles and on foot who were all about, did not see that the rock looked at all different.

"A fine place for us it will make," said the King; "we couldn't be asking for a better. Get to work now, all of you. Hollow out the inside of the hill, only leave pillars to hold up the roof, and go and find gold for the floor and silver for the walls, and you can have every other pillar gold and every other one silver, after you get the rest done, and take down the rock that you left. And then find diamonds and rubies and emeralds to light it with."

No, I am not going to explain to you how the fairies did all this. I shall not tell you how they got the rock out nor what they did with it after they got it out. I will tell you all that there is any need of your knowing about it, and that is that in a very short time it was all done; that the new fairy palace was as much larger and finer and better than any fairy palace in Ireland ever was as we Americans intend that everything here shall be larger and finer and better than anything anywhere else. And it was all done before the most of the messengers who had been sent in other directions got back to tell what they had found.

These fairies went straight to where the O'Briens lived, and there the fairies who had been left on guard told them where to find the King, and asked them to say to him that they were tired of their duty and they wished that he could send somebody else to take their places.

The fairies were not much surprised when they found the King and all the tribe settled in a new palace, as comfortably as if they had never moved. The building of a palace in a night is no more to a fairy than it is to a New York man to come back after he has been out of town for a month and find a house twenty stories high in a place where there was a hole in the ground when he went away.

"What's the use at all to be tellin' Your Majesty what we've found in the places we've been," said one of the first who came back, "and you livin' this minute in the finest palace that was ever dug out of a hill?"

"You may tell us all the same," said the King.

"Well and good," said the fairy. "It's to the south I've been. First there's all this island that we're on, down to the place with the grass and the iron chain around it. Then there's the bay, with the ships. Then there's another island, with hills and trees, and then there's the sea, and a long shore, all sand, and hundreds of houses, big and little, where people live. And that's all."

Another fairy said: "I went farther to the west than this, but not much farther till I came to a great river. Of course I couldn't be crossin' the runnin' water, so I went round the mouth of it and then kept on. The country was all flat for a good way, and bars of iron everywhere, laid two and two, so many of them that I didn't dare rest anywhere, and there were towns and plenty of people, and then at long last I came to hills."

I suppose you know, without my telling you, that fairies cannot bear to cross running water, any more than they can bear to touch iron, and that was why this fairy had to go around the mouth of the Hudson River instead of going across it.

Then came another fairy, who had been to the north, and he said: "It beats everything, the lovely country I've seen. Never a better did I see anywhere. Hills and woods and mountains, and the trees all yellow and red and green and brown. I went up the big river on this side for a long way, and then I saw great mountains on the other side. So beautiful they looked, I wanted to go to them, only, sure, I couldn't cross the river. So I went round the head of it and came down back to the mountains. And there I found that they were full of fairies already. But they seemed to be Dutch, and it's little English they could talk, let alone Irish. Still we got along, and they gave me some mighty fine drink that they had. And they said that we could come there, the whole tribe, and welcome kindly, and I'ld say it was a good place to go, only it's farther off than this from them we want to be near."

"We'll stay where we are," said the King. "It's as well that we know what's all around us, but here we'll be more to ourselves, as many people as there are, for I'm thinkin' there's no fairies but us here."

Then slowly out of the crowd of fairies one came forward and said: "Your Majesty, could I be saying something that's breakin' my heart? It's hard for me to say and it'll maybe be harder for you to hear; but it's on my mind and I can't get it off my mind. Will you forgive me if I say it?"

And the King answered: "It's much that's bad and a little that's good we've heard since we left our own home. But it's best that we know all there is to know, bad or good. Say what you have to say."

"It's not far I've been," said the fairy; "only around here in the city that's all about us; but many things I've seen, and wonderful things. Ah, Your Majesty, don't blame me for what I'm saying, but what's to become of us all and of you yourself, I dunno. We know all about magic; we've known all about it for years — aye, for ages. And we thought that made us better than mortals. We thought they could never do the things we could do; maybe they never can. But oh, Your Majesty, they're doing things as good as we can do, or better. You wouldn't believe what the mortals in this country do, if you wasn't after seein' it. They do things as wonderful as we ourselves, and it's iron, iron, iron everywhere. We can do nothing with iron — we can't touch it — and what will we do at all to be ahead of them, or even up with them?"

"What's all this they do?" said the King.

"You saw yourself," the fairy said, "the coaches that went along up in the air. They go on bridges, miles long, built of iron. And they run on bars of iron. You saw for yourself that they had no horses, and the coach in front that pulls them is all made of iron, and men ride in them, as if it was no harm at all to touch iron. And that's not all. There are other coaches that go in the streets without horses. They have no iron coach in front to pull them. They go in different ways. Sometimes there's an iron rope, that's all the time moving and moving along under the street, and there's a gripping iron under the coach that takes hold on it, and so it's pulled along. And sometimes there's only a little string — not iron, I think, but some other metal — and something just reaches down from the coach and touches it, and that makes it go. I dunno how it is, but it makes it go. And sometimes there's fire comes out of it."

Then another fairy came out of the crowd and stood before the King. "Your Majesty," he said, "I can tell you more than that. I have been about the city, too, and I went into some of the houses. I saw a man talking to a little box on the wall. I came close and I heard that the box was talking to him too. I thought there was a fairy inside it, but I looked inside, and there was nothing there but iron and strange works that I couldn't understand. There were little strings of copper coming out of the box, and then a long string of iron, that led away over the tops of the houses."

The fairy stopped and shivered as he thought of the horrible string of iron. Then he went on: "I followed it and it came into another house, where there was so much iron that I couldn't stay there. But the strings of iron came out of this house and led in all directions. I followed them and I listened everywhere and I found what they were for, though how they do it all I dunno. And it's this way: Anywhere that there's a box you can talk to them that's in the house where all the iron strings go. And if they like to help you, you can talk to anybody else where there's a box. It may be a mile off or it may be a dozen miles off. Many a time those in the house where all the strings are will not help them that wants to talk, but when they will, it's easy. Yes, Your Majesty, one man talks to another ten miles off, as if he was standing by his side."

"Your Majesty," said another fairy, "you saw yourself the bright lights that were at the place where the grass was, that we came to first, and you've seen thousands more of them since. Do you know that they're not candles, and they're not lamps, and that there's no fire to them at all? There's strings of something, whatever it is, from one of them to another, and the light goes through that, whatever it is."

"There's another thing that they do with strings like that," said still another fairy. "I saw men doing it not far from here. They made a hole in a rock and they put one end of a string in it. Then where the other end was, a man pushed a thing like a sort of handle, and the rock was all burst open, and nobody had touched it."

And another fairy said: "Your Majesty, there are boats all the time going across the rivers — across the running water. Of course we always knew that mortals could cross running water, but these boats go without sails or oars, like the ship that we came here on. To be sure I couldn't go on one, because it was across running water, but I went near one, when it was at the shore, and it was all full of iron, and I got the most awful pains from being near it. It was as bad, almost, as I felt coming here, when I'ld get too near the iron sides of the ship."

"And a strange thing it was that I saw too," said another fairy. "I saw people looking into little boxes of wood, so I looked in too. And in one I saw a woman dancing, and in another there were horses running, and in another I saw two men fighting. And it was not a real woman or real horses or real men, but only pictures that moved and did the things that real people and horses would do."

The King listened to all this and then he sat and thought. "What is there in it that I can't do?" he asked. "Do you not all know of the coaches in Ireland that are drawn by horses without heads and driven by coachmen without heads?"

All the fairies looked at one another and nodded and said, "Yes, yes, we know."

But Naggeneen came forward and stood before the throne. Nobody had noticed that he had been listening or that he was there. "And what if those coaches were in Ireland?" he said. "They had horses, though the horses had no heads. Can you make iron coaches go without any horses at all?"

The King was trying to talk boldly, but he stammered and grew pale at the very thought of having anything to do with an iron coach, and he did not answer. He went on instead: "Can I not send any one of you on a message, as fast as the wind?"

"But can you talk for ten miles," Naggeneen asked, "and will the very voice of you go as fast as the lightning?"

"Why would I want to be doin' that," said the King, "when I can send a messenger as fast as I like?"

"That's not the question," said the cruel Naggeneen; "can you do it?"

"I never tried," said the King. "And can I not light up this palace," he went on, "or any other palace, with diamonds? Can I not make a light so that a man who looks behind him when he is going on a journey or at work in the fields will think his house is on fire and run back?"

"And when he has run back," said Naggeneen, "will he find that his house is on fire? You know that he will not. It's only glamour, and he'll soon be laughing at you. Oh, we can catch a few firebugs in spiders' webs and deceive a boy or a girl that's passing, and maybe make them turn aside and dance with us, but can you put real lights all over the country for miles — lights that will burn on and on and show real things? Our lights are lies themselves and they can no more than lead a silly mortal astray for a time; their lights tell the truth. What else can you do?"

The King had lost the most of his boldness. "They say," he said, "that men can burst open the rock. Can I not do that as well?"

"You can open this rock for us to pass through," said Naggeneen; "and what then? A man can see it open for a moment, if you choose to let him, and the next minute it's all as one as if you had never touched it. And the man thinks that's wonderful, for he doesn't know that you can do it no other way. All glamour again! Can you burst the rock open and leave it open, so that it will always be so, for mortal and for fairy?"

"Why should I want to be doin' that?" said the King.

"For the same reason makes the men want to do it, but you couldn't. And those boats that cross the river, full of iron — can you make them, and can you cross the running water in them?"

The King had no voice to answer. "And the pictures in the boxes," Naggeneen went on; "can you make pictures dance?"

"Sure," said the King, "I can make a man think he sees anything I like — a woman dancing or a horse running, or anything."

"Glamour! Glamour! Glamour!" cried Naggeneen. "You can make him think he sees! Yes, but he does not see. You can no more make a picture dance than you can cross a river!" And Naggeneen turned on his heel and walked off, as if he thought the King a poor creature that was not worth talking to.

The King had no more courage left in him than if he had been talking to the King of All Ireland instead of to Naggeneen. "Naggeneen," he cried, "come back and tell us something better nor all this. It's not pleasant you are in your talk, and it's often you make me angry with you, but after all you're cleverer than any of us. Tell us what to do. It was not like this where we lived before. There we could do all manner of things that mortals could not, and they were afraid of us."

"And so here too," said Naggeneen, "you can do all manner of things that mortals cannot, but they can do as many that you cannot — as many and better."

"But what are we to do," the King went on, 'to show them that we're their masters? Sure we're cleverer than them all out, and we can prove it in some way."

"King," said Naggeneen, speaking as boldly as if he were himself a greater king, "you can never prove that you're cleverer than men, for you're not cleverer. It was a poor, wasted, weak, and sorrowful country that we came from, and its a rich, new, strong, and happy country that we've come to. There's the differ. Clever you are, maybe, and your people, too, and I may be clever in my own way, and we may play our little tricks on mortals, as I did on the Sullivans, if they're as stupid as them. But mortals can be cleverer than we ever can when they are clever, and they can beat us every time if they know how. And do you know why? Because they have what we have not — because they have souls. I heard a school-master say once that the word 'mortal' was made from a word that meant death. And they call mortals that, I'm thinkin', because they never die. But you will die, King, and all your people, and I. We live on and on for thousands of years, and men come and change and pass away, but at the last day we shall be gone, as a bit of cloud up in the sky is gone when the sun shines on it. That's why men will always be greater and finer and stronger than us, with all our magic."

The fairies were all so terrified that they shrank away from Naggeneen and clung together and shook, in their fright, for this fear of living for a long time and then going out like a candle is their greatest fear. There was not a bit of color left in the King's face now. It was almost with a sob that he spoke again, and there was a kind of beseeching in his tone as he said: "Naggeneen, don't talk like that to us! We don't know it! It may be so, but we don't know it! We've tried many a time to find out, but no one that knew would ever tell us! We may have souls! We don't know that we've not! We may be saved!"

"You do know it!" Naggeneen cried. "Why will you try to deceive yourselves? You've no soul and I've no soul, and there's no way that we can have them. If there'd been any way, I'ld have had one long ago. But we'll never have them, and mortals will always outwit us, if they half know how. Shall I tell you how one of them outwitted me — a big, lazy, stupid gommoch, with not enough brains to keep his neck safe?"

The fairies were far past caring whether they heard a story or not, but they listened as Naggeneen went on. "I'm after tellin' you," he said, "that if there was any way that one of us could be gettin' a soul, I'ld have had one long ago. This was the way I tried it, and a silly mortal outwitted me. Guleesh na Guss Dhu was the name that was on him. I had heard — and I believed it — that if I could get a mortal woman married to me — a woman with a soul — that I would get a soul, too, that way. Well, I was never over-modest in my tastes, you know, and I thought that the daughter of the King of France was about right for me. A beautiful girl she was, with the rose and the lily fighting in her cheeks, and she was eighteen years old. But sure I thought that the differ of a few thousand years in our ages would be nothing to me, and I hoped it would be nothing to her either.

"I was living in a rath and wearing a green jacket then. All the others in the rath promised that they'ld help me. The King's daughter was to be married to the son of the King of another country on November Eve; and you know there's no better time to steal a girl than the night she's to be married, and November Eve is a fine time, too, so it was settled that we'ld go over to France and steal her on that night. But, as you know, we needed a mortal to help us. How else could we be bringin' her across from France? If we could put her on a horse behind a man, she'ld have flesh and blood to take a grip of, but if she was put up behind one of us, she might as well try to hold to a puff of smoke. You know that.

"We got ready, making sure that we'ld find some fool of a mortal ready for us when the time came, and sure enough, when we'd been out for a little look at the country before starting, and were coming back, there sat this same Guleesh na Guss Dhu, between the rath and the gable of his father's house, that was near by, staring up at the moon, like he'd never seen one before. There was no need to try to catch him or to bring him with us, or the likes of that. All we had to do was to let him hear us as we passed and let him see the door of the rath open, and in he came of him-self to see what it was all about. We hadn't let him see ourselves yet, but he heard us all calling: 'My horse and bridle and saddle! My horse and bridle and saddle!' and what did he do but call out after us: 'My horse and bridle and saddle!'

"There was the beam of a plough lying near, and I changed it into a horse for him, and pleased he was when he saw it standing forninst him, with its bridle of gold and saddle of silver and all. The minute he saw it he jumped on it, and then we let him see all ourselves and our horses, and he nearly fell off again, with the sight of the crowd of us.

"Then I said to him: 'Are you coming with us to-night, Guleesh?'

"'I am,' he said.

"And with that we set off, and we overtook the wind that was before us, and the wind that was behind us did not overtake us. And we never stopped till we came to the sea. Then every one of us said: 'Hie over cap! Hie over cap!' and Guleesh said it after us, and the next second we was all up in the air, and we never stopped till we was in Rome. And why the whole tribe wanted to go by the way of Rome, never a know I know, for it's not on the way from Ireland to the palace of the King of France at all.

"Then I spoke up to Guleesh and says I: 'Do you know why we brought you here?' says I. 'The daughter of the King of France is to be married this night, and we mean to carry her off, and we need you so that she can sit behind you on the horse, for you are flesh and blood and she'll have something to hold to. Will you do that for us now?'

"'I'll do whatever you say,' says Guleesh; 'and where are we now, if you please?'

"'We're in Rome,' says I.

"'Oh, in Rome is it?' says Guleesh. 'Sure, then, I'm glad of that. The priest of our parish lost his place a little while ago, only because they said he drank too much, as if there'ld be any harm in that, and now is the fine time to go to the Pope and get a bull to put him back in his place.'

"'Ah, we've no time for that, Guleesh,' says I, 'and we must be gettin' to the palace of the King of France before we lose any more.'

"'Not a foot will I go,' says Guleesh, 'till I get the bull for the priest. You can go on and leave me here if you like, and you can stop for me when you come back.'

"Well, we had more talk about it, and then one of the others says: 'Sure, Naggeneen, we can't go without him and we can't get him to come with us, so we'll have to try to get the Pope's bull for him. Go with him to the Pope and help him all you can, and we'll wait for you.'

"'Come with me, then,' says I, and I took him by the hand, and before he knew how I did it, I had him in the room where the Pope was. The Pope was sitting by himself, reading a book, and he had a tumbler of hot whiskey, with a little bit of sugar, beside him on the table, all as comfortable as you please. 'Now, Guleesh,' says I, 'ask him for the bull, and tell him that if he won't give it to you, you'll set the house on fire. Then leave the rest to me.'

"So Guleesh walked up to him as bold as you please, and when the Pope saw him he was near scared to death, because he thought that nobody could get into the room where he was. Then Guleesh says to him: 'Don't be afraid, Your Honor; all I want of you is your bull to put our parish priest back in his place, that lost it some time ago, because somebody told lies about him and said that he drank too much. And when I have your bull I'll be leavin' you in peace again.'

"'Go on out o' this,' says the Pope; 'where are all my servants?' and he began calling for them, but Guleesh put his back against the door, so that nobody could open it on the other side, and then he began telling the Pope all about the priest, and the Pope had nothing to do but listen.

"And when he was done the Pope refused up and down to give him any pardon for the priest. 'Then,' says Guleesh, 'unless you give it to me at once I'll burn your house.' And with that I began blowing fire out of my mouth all around the room.

"'Oh, stop the fire,' cries the Pope, 'and I'll give you the pardon or anything else you ask!'

"So then I stopped the fire, and the Pope sat down and wrote the pardon for the priest, giving him back his old place, and gave it to Guleesh. That second I caught him by the hand and we were off again through the keyhole to where the other fairies were. In another minute we were all on our horses and away again. We overtook the wind that was before us, and the wind that was behind us did not overtake us till we were at the palace of the King of France. And there my fine boy Guleesh saw sights that he never saw the like of before.

"The place was almost as fine as this of yours here. There were long tables all about it, with everything on them that a body would be wanting to eat and drink, and as fast as any of it was eaten or drunk, there was more put in its place. Then there were hundreds of noblemen and ladies, all in clothes of silk and velvet and gold and silver, and all covered with jewels, till they shone in the light of the gold chandeliers, almost like they'd been chandeliers themselves. And they were talking and laughing and singing and playing, and some of them were dancing — not so well as we dance, of course, when we've a mind, but enough to make Guleesh think he was seeing the grandest sight that ever was in the world entirely. And up at one end of the hall was an altar and two bishops, ready to marry the Princess to the King's son as soon as it would be the right time.

"'And which of them all is the Princess?' says Guleesh to me.

"'That one there near to ye,' says I, pointing her out."

Naggeneen stopped in his story and seemed to forget for a moment that he was telling it. "Oh, but she was the beauty of the world!" he went on, speaking so low that the fairies could scarcely hear him. "There was the lily and the rose in her cheeks, and her arms like snow, and her hair like soft gold. Not like the gold that you dig out of the ground for your palace, but gold with life in it. And her eyes were like two big violets with the dew on them. And there stood the others all around her, all merry and happy, and she —

"'What is she crying for?' says Guleesh to me. 'Sure it's not right that eyes like those would have tears in them.'

"'True for you, it's not, Guleesh,' said I, 'and it's because there's no love in her heart for the man that she's to be married to. It's her father that's compelling her, for he has some arrangement of the sort with the other King, that's the father of the young man. And it's for that,' I said, 'that we're going to carry her off, and it's the best thing we could be doing for her as well as ourselves.'

"Just that minute the young Prince came and offered her his hand, and away they went in the dance, and the tears in her eyes all the time. And as soon as the dance was over, the King, her father, and the Queen, her mother, came and said that it was time they were married, and the two bishops waiting there all the time. So they led the Prince and the Princess up toward the altar, and she with the rose all gone out of her cheeks and only the lily left. But when they were not more than four yards from the altar I put out my foot before the Princess, and she fell, and then, with a word of a charm, I made her invisible to all but Guleesh and ourselves. Then I made a sign to Guleesh, and he took up the Princess and ran with her out of the hall, and all the rest of us after them. 'My horse and bridle and saddle!' says every one of us, and the same says Guleesh. He lifted the Princess up behind him on his horse and we were away again. We overtook the wind that was before us, and the wind that was behind us did not overtake us till we came to the sea. 'Hie over cap!' cried every one of us, and 'Hie over cap!' cried Guleesh, and in a moment we were in Ireland again.

"Another minute and we were close to our own rath, and it was then that all the work of the night was lost. For then what did

the fool Guleesh do but take the Princess in his arms and leap
down off his horse, and he cried: 'I call you to myself, in the name
of — ' Oh, now, you little cowards, you've no call to shrink away
like that and to try to be hiding in the dark corners! You know I
can't say the name that he said. But he said it, and then the enchantment was all gone, and he saw that the horse he'd been riding was nothing but the beam of a plough and that the horse that
each of the others had was only an old broom, or maybe a rag
weed, or the like of that.

"And you know that there was no getting the Princess away
from him after the words that he said. But I came close to her and
struck her on the mouth. 'Now, Guleesh,' said I, 'you may keep
her if you will, but she'll be dumb forever.' And with that we all
disappeared from them.

"But you may be sure I watched them. They stood there together and Guleesh talked to her and tried to make her talk back,
but it was of no use at all, and he soon found that she was dumb
completely. Then he stood thinking what would he do with her,
and at last he took her by the hand and started toward the priest's
house. It was getting near day now, and the priest was up by the
time they came to the door, and he opened it himself. And when
he saw Guleesh and the girl, sure he thought they were come to
be married, and he said: 'Ah, Guleesh, isn't it the nice boy ye are,
that ye can't wait till a decent hour to be married, but ye must be
comin' to me this early? And don't ye know I can't marry ye law-
fully anyway, and I put out of my place?'

"HERE'S THE POPE'S BULL FOR THAT SAME."

"Then says Guleesh: 'Sure, father, you can marry me or anybody else you like, for you have your place back again, and here's the Pope's bull for that same. But it's not that I come for, but to ask you to give shelter to this young lady, the daughter of the King of France.'

"And with that he takes the Pope's bull out of his pocket and gives it to the priest, and the priest looked at the writing and the seal and saw that there was no doubt but it was right. And so he made Guleesh and the Princess come in and sit down, while Guleesh told him the whole story, and not a word of it would he have believed only there was the Pope's bull that he couldn't deny, and so at long last he had to believe all that Guleesh told him. And the end of it was that the Princess stayed at the priest's house, for they didn't know how to send her back to her father's palace, and they had no money, and she couldn't speak to help them. And the priest gave out that she was the daughter of his brother, that lived in another county, and that she was making him a visit. And Guleesh went home and said how he'd been sleeping beside the rath all night."

Naggeneen paused in his story, while all the fairies drew quietly closer to him. "Do you see," he said, "how I was tricked by a fool of a mortal? Oh, she was the beauty of the world, and he took her from me with a word, as easily as you'd steal the butter out of a churn. And that was not all.

"I said to myself that I was not done with my revenge on them yet. She could not speak and it was a sore punishment on the both of them. Yet she stayed on at the priest's house. The priest wrote letters to her father, as I heard, and gave them to merchants who were travelling, but none of them ever reached him. And Guleesh got mighty serious about his soul all at once, so that he had to be at the priest's house every day, and every day he saw the Princess. She could never talk to him, but she learned to make signs that he could understand. And so it went on for a year.

"And then, when it was November Eve again, and we had been out of the rath and were all coming into it again in a great crowd, there sat Guleesh, the same as before. He couldn't see us, but he must have heard us, for you could see that he was listening with all his ears. And I thought now was the fine time to be having the laugh on him. By that time everybody was shouting: 'My horse and bridle and saddle! My horse and bridle and saddle!' and Guleesh shouted as before: 'My horse and bridle and saddle! My horse and bridle and saddle!'

"'Now is my chance to be even with him,' thought I, and I said: 'Ah, Guleesh, my boy, is that yourself that's to the fore again? You'll get no horse to-night and you'll play no more tricks on us. How are you getting on with your Princess? Does she talk to you much? Or do you just like to sit and look at her?'

"And when I said that, he looked so pale and so sad that I almost screamed with joy, and I couldn't keep myself from whispering to the man that was next to me: 'And isn't he the stupid omadhaun, not to know that there's an herb growing close to his own door that would give her back her speech if he'd only boil it and give it to her?'

"'It's the stupid omadhaun he is,' said the other man.

"Oh, and it was me that was the omadhaun, to be saying it at all. Oh, why couldn't I hold my jaw? But it was like some spell was on me, and I had to say it. I had to say it! I couldn't have kept it back if I'd tried. And he heard every word!

"It's little more there is to tell. The next morning, as soon as there was light, there was Guleesh searching for any herb that was strange to him around the door. And it was not long till he found it. Then he boiled it, and he drank some of it himself, to see whether it might be poison, and it put him into a deep sleep. And when he woke he went to the priest's house and told the whole story and gave the Princess some of the drink, and then she went to sleep and did not wake till the next day. And when she woke she had her speech back.

"Ah, well, by this time they was both in love with each other, and all that I did for myself or against them had only helped them. But it was not long before the Princess was saying that she must be off to her father, and nothing that the priest and Guleesh could do would make her stay. So the priest took the jewels that she had on her when Guleesh first brought her, and he sold them and gave her the money, and she took it and paid her way back to France.

"And after that great grief and melancholy came over Guleesh, and nothing would do him but he must start off for France to find the Princess again. Start off he did, and that was the last that I ever saw of him, only I heard that he found the Princess at her father's court and that at long last they were married."

There was nothing strange in the last that Naggeneen had told — nothing more strange, I mean, than that a peasant boy should marry the daughter of the King of France — but his voice, before he had ended, was so low and so full of grief that all the other fairies kept very still to listen, and when he had told his story none of them spoke for a little while. At last the King said: "How long was all this ago, Naggeneen?"

"Many years," Naggeneen answered; "I couldn't be counting how many."

73

"Then what is it to you now?" said the King. "Sure they're both dead long ago, and here are you as sound as ever."

"Yes," Naggeneen cried, "as sound as ever and as sound as I'll ever be. They're not dead. They had souls. They're alive now, and when what they call 'the Last Day' comes, they'll live still, forever. And then I shall go out, like a shadow when the light falls on it. There's no more of me that can last than a shadow. And you will go out that way, too, and all of us. It was not her that I wanted so much. It was the soul that I thought I'ld get, and her married to me. That was it. And a stupid mortal had tricked me twice. It was then I left the rath. It was then I could bear to look at nobody, man or fairy. Then I put on the red jacket and went by myself. After a time I was a lepracaun, and a cluricaun, and nothing at all, as it suited me, and sometimes I lived in a rath with others, as I have in yours, and other times I went by myself. But I never forgot how I was tricked by a mortal, and I've never forgot how I missed getting a soul when I was near to it.

"You've never liked me; you've always thought me sour and harsh and cruel. Do you see why now? Since that time I've always hated all men, because of the one that tricked me; and I've always hated all women, because of the one I lost; and I've always hated all fairies, because they are all as weak and helpless and pitiful as myself. I hate myself and I hate all of you, because there's no good for any of us in all the world forever."

"Naggeneen," said the King, "we've never been too fond of you, it's true, but maybe we'ld have liked you better if you'd told us this before. But you're cleverer than all of us. Tell us what we'll do now, so that these mortals won't be getting the better of us all out."

"What'll you do?" Naggeneen answered; "there's nothing you can do. They'll outwit you, whatever you do."

"But there must be some way. Tell us what to do, Naggeneen," the King pleaded.

"I'll tell you what to do, then,' said Naggeneen; "send out your people and let them learn the ways of men. Let them learn to make the iron coaches that go up in the air; let them learn to make the coaches that go on the ground, with the iron ropes; let them learn to talk miles away through iron strings; let them learn to make the bright lights that you see; let them learn to open the rock so that it will not close again; let them learn to cross running water in boats full of iron; let them learn to handle iron and do what they like with it, as if it were only gold, and then, maybe, they'll be able to do all the things that men do."

The fairies were simply cowering away from the King and Naggeneen and shivering and squealing with fright at the talk of handling iron and crossing running water. "Ah, Naggeneen," said the King, "you know we can't do all that. Tell us what we'll do at all."

"There's nothing that you can do," said Naggeneen. "There's only one thing I know you can try, and I think that'll do no good either."

"But what is it?" said the King. "We'll try it, anyway."

"It's not the time to try it yet," Naggeneen answered. "When the time comes I'll tell you."

"Then, Naggeneen," said the King, "give us a tune out of the fiddle."

And Naggeneen took the fiddle and played. But there was no merriment in it now. It was only the breath of sorrow and loss and disappointment that breathed from the shivering strings. The fairies did not dance; they only stood and listened, pale and still. In a few moments the King gave the sign for Naggeneen to stop, and in a minute more the lights were out and the whole palace was as quiet as the hill, before any palace was there.

V.
THE TIME FOR NAGGENEEN'S PLAN

Little happened that needs to be told in the next few months, either to the fairies or to the human people. John O'Brien and Peter Sullivan were not long in finding work to do, and they were paid for it, and the two families got on better than they had in Ireland. The O'Briens got on better than the Sullivans. John was a better workman than Peter. Peter could do the work that was set before him in the way that he was told. But John could do better than that. He could see for himself how the work ought to be done, and he saw that if he did it well he might get better work to do. In Ireland, work as he would, he could no more than live, and so he had come to care little what he did or how he did it. But it was different here. The men who employed him saw that he was not a common workman, and soon they gave him better than the common work and more than the common pay.

But Peter was a common workman. Then, too, John's mother knew how to care for the house better than Ellen did, and because of that, too, the O'Briens did better. Every day, just as she used to do in Ireland, Mrs. O'Brien left something to eat and drink outside the house for the Good People. She said that she did not know whether there were any Good People here, but if there were they must be well treated. And when she found that what she left for them was taken, she said that she knew that there were Good People here. Of course she did not know that they were the same ones who had lived near them in Ireland. She put the milk and the water and the bread, or whatever she had for them, on the fire-escape, at the back of the rooms where they lived. And first she always laid down a little piece of carpet to put the dishes on, so that the fairies could come and get the food without touching the iron, for she knew that they could never do that. There was only one thing that did not go well with the O'Briens. Kitty's health did not come back to her, as they had hoped that it would. She did not need to do any work now, though she would do some, and the rest was good for her, but she was still pale and still weak.

Though the Sullivans did not find their fortunes so much improved in the new country as the O'Briens did, yet they felt that they had gained, too, and in one way especially. For the King of the fairies had forbidden Naggeneen to trouble them any more. Naggeneen asked what for at all he had come over all the sea, if he was not to trouble the Sullivans. The King was always ready enough to have Naggeneen's help, when he thought that his cleverness would be of use; but there were times when he would be obeyed, and this was one of them, so Naggeneen had to do as he was told.

The King tried all the things that Naggeneen had told him to do, to make his people learn all the wonderful magic that the human people knew so well. Naggeneen had told him at first that it would all be of no use, and so the King found it. The fairies were sent out to watch the men, to see all that they did, and to learn how to do it. It was all in vain.

The King often asked Naggeneen what was the one other way that he had said they might try. Naggeneen would never tell. When the time came to try it, he said, he would tell what it was, but it would be of no more use than the rest that they had done. Naggeneen laughed at all the others when they came home baffled and out of sorts. "You'll never do the things that men do," he said, "any more than they'll ever do the things that you do. And their wonders are more and better than yours."

After a time they ceased to try to learn any more. They began to live much as they had lived in Ireland. They had found a green place where they could dance, near the palace, but it was winter now, and the snow was over everything much of the time. They went to the O'Briens every day for the food that was left outside the window for them, and, for the most part, they spent the rest of the time in the palace. Often Naggeneen played the fiddle or the pipes for them. Then they forgot that it was his fault that they had ever come here, but when he stopped playing they remembered it and hated him again. And Naggeneen laughed at them. He had a strange laugh, without a bit of merriment or good-humor in it. There was something sad in his laugh and something sour, but nothing that it was pleasant to hear.

Then the spring began to come. The grass was looking a bit green and the air was warmer. They could dance on the grass now, whenever they liked. They had given up trying to learn the ways of men, and they were beginning to feel as if they had always lived here. Then Naggeneen came one evening and stood before the King and said: "It is the time now to try my plan, if you want to try it, but it's no good."

"What's the plan, then, at all?" the King asked.

"You know well," said Naggeneen, "that your people can find out nothing by going out and watching what men do. Now, what you want is to get a human child here, or maybe two of them, and keep them and let them grow up with you here, and then send them out to learn everything that men do, and come back and teach it to your people. Then you'll learn all these things that men do, and you can do the like."

"Ah, Naggeneen," said the King, "it's yourself was always the clever boy. We'll do that same."

"You will so," Naggeneen replied, "and no good will it ever do you. I've told you before and I tell you again, you'll never do the things that men do. But it's crazy you are to try all ways, and I have to be telling you the ways to try. Go on and do it, if it divarts you."

"And where'll we get the human child at all?" the Queen asked.

"Sure then," said Naggeneen, "and haven't you heard the news? Why, there's a baby at the Sullivans' since this morning, and one at the O'Briens' since this afternoon. The one at the Sullivans' is a boy and the one at the O'Briens' is a girl. Go and get them and leave two of your own people in their places. You know how to do that; it's nothing new to you."

"Take a child from the O'Briens!" the Queen cried. "From them that's always been so good to us and always given us the bit and sup, when they scarcely had it themselves? I'd never do such a thing."

"But you'd be leaving one of your own people in the place of it," Naggeneen answered, "and they'ld never know the differ. Or if they did, it would be no matter. A woman makes a great hulla-baloo when her child looks sick and she thinks it's dying on her, but she doesn't care at all after a little. And then, it doesn't die, and she thinks it's her own child all the time, and there's no harm done. And His Majesty here thinks it's going to do a power of good for all of you. It's not, but he thinks it is."

"We'll never take a child from the O'Briens if I can help it," the Queen said. "From the Sullivans I don't care, but not from the O'Briens."

"We'll have to do it," said the King. "I don't like to hurt the O'Briens myself, but it's for the good of us all, and it's our only chance. These mortals are getting ahead of us that far, and they'll be doing something next that will exterminate us entirely. We'll send and get both the children."

The Queen urged again that the O'Briens had always been good to the Good People and must not be harmed, but the King had his mind set on Naggeneen's plan and he would hear of nothing else. It was settled and it could not be changed. They must have both children. They should live among the fairies till they were old enough to be sent out to learn the ways of men. And they should always come back and teach the fairies the ways of men that they had learned.

"And it's to-night we'd better be doing it, if we're to do it at all," said the King. "Now, who'll be the ones to go and be put in the place of the children?"

Nobody seemed to care about going to play the part of a baby with the Sullivans, or even with the O'Briens. Everybody was trying to get out of the King's sight behind the others. "We'ld have to be lyin' still all day," one whispered, "with never a dance to rest ourselves with."

"They might be puttin' holy water on us," said another, and all who heard him shivered.

"There'll be all sorts of unpleasantness, anyway," said a third.

"Maybe they'ld find us out," said a fourth, "and then they'ld be puttin' all sorts of horrible charms on us to be rid of us."

But the King called one of the women and told her that she must go and stay in the place of the baby at the O'Briens. She whimpered a little, but she knew that what the King said must be done. Then the King looked around him and said, "Where's Naggeneen got to at all now?"

"Here I am to the fore," said Naggeneen.

"You'll go," said the King, "and you'll be put in the place of the boy that's at the Sullivans."

"I go!" said Naggeneen. "Never a step. Didn't I tell you of the plan? And that's enough. Now do it for yourself. I don't belong to you and you know it. Do your own work."

"I'll not be disputin' with you," said the King. "Whether you belong to me or no, you're in my palace along with my tribe, and you'll do what I tell you. It's tired of you I've been this great while, and now I've a chance to be rid of you. You'll go to the Sullivans and you'll stay there and you'll grow up like their child. And mind you play your part well and don't let them know what you are. If you do, they'll work some charm on you and be rid of you, and then we'll have to send back the real child, and all your own plan will be lost."

"And how will you carry out my plan without me?" Naggeneen asked. "Don't I always tell you what to do? You'll want me a dozen times a day."

"We'll not want you at all. You do tell us what to do and we do it when we like, and it's small good ever came of it. And then, if we do want anything of you, we know where to find you, and we'll easily come to you. It's been done before. You was left in the place of a young man that was taken away once before, and when the tribe that you was with then wanted to talk to you they came to you, and we can do the same if we like, but I don't think we shall like."

"That's just it," Naggeneen cried; "did you know about that time? This time would be just like it. Do you know how they drove me off? I couldn't help it then and I couldn't help it again. There's times when it seems like there's a charm on me, and so there is, belike, and I have to do a thing that it's bad for me to do. Do you know the whole of it, how it was that time?

"It was a man that time, as you say, and not a child. Rickard the Rake he was called, I remember, and a fine rake he was. Never a bit of work would he do, but he'ld always be at every fair or wake or the like of that. And so little good there was in him that the fairies in the rath where I was then said: 'It's an easy thing it'll be stealing him away, and serve him right, too, and he'll be handy for us, he's so good a dancer.'

"I was ordered to be the one to be left in his place, though I knew no good would come of it. And so one night, when he was dancing, we struck him with a dart in the hip, and he fell down where he was. And then, in all the bother and the noise that there was, it was easy to get him away and to leave me in the place of him. So they took me up and put me in bed and nursed me and did all they could think of for me, and me all the time squirming and squealing, like it was dying I was.

"They gave me everything I could think of to eat, and that was not so bad, for I never lived better in my life; but it was worn out I was getting, with lying there all the time and playing sick, and never a chance to stir about or get any air or a minute to myself. And the thing I was spoiling for was a tune out of the pipes or the fiddle. Then they brought a fairy-man to look at me, and he said it was a fairy and not Rickard at all that was in it, and I couldn't be telling you all the bad names he put on me and the things he said about me. And he said: 'Leave a pair of bagpipes near him, and maybe he'll play them. You know well Rickard never could play at all, and so if he plays them we'll know that it's not Rickard, but a fairy changeling, and then we'll know what to do.'"

Just here I must stop Naggeneen in his story for a minute, to tell you that when people in Ireland speak of a "fairy-man" they do not mean a man fairy. They mean a man who knows all about fairies. The fairy-men know all that the fairies can do, and they know the charms against them and the ways to cure a sickness that the fairies have brought upon anyone, and the ways to keep them from stealing the cream from the milk and the milk from the cow. So the people have great respect for a fairy-man or a fairy-woman, and they often send to one of them for help, when they think that the fairies may have done them a mischief.

"They left the pipes beside me," Naggeneen went on, "and then they went away. Oh, it was then I had the terrible time all out. Oh, may I never long for anything again as I longed to play them pipes! But I knew that they'ld be listening and watching, and if I caught me at it, I'ld have to pay for it, if they could make me. So I kept my hands off them and only groaned and took on as if the dart in my hip was killing me entirely.

"Then there was one hot afternoon, and everything was still about the house, and it was the harvest time, and they all had a right to be in the fields at work. And sure I thought it was there they were. And then the wish to play the pipes came on me worse than ever before. And it was then that it was like there was a charm on me, as I was telling you. I had to do what I did. I could no more help doing it than a girl can help dancing with us, when we get her in our ring on May Eve. But first I opened the door a crack and looked out into the kitchen, to see was there anybody there, and there was nobody. But they were all in another room, as I found out after, waiting and listening. There was the fairy-man and a fairy-woman and all the people of the house, and some of the neighbors.

"But if I'd seen them all I dunno if I could have done other than I did, the power, whatever it was, was on me that strong. And I took the pipes and played. It was soft I played at first, and then the music got the better of me and I went on more and louder, and I played tunes and tunes. I could play as well then as I can now, and so the other fairies, that had been without me for some time, must have heard me playing, for soon I heard the rustle and the whisper and the patter of their coming, and then they gathered round me, and I had been left there lonely for so long that I kept on playing, to keep them with me.

"It was then the fairy-man and the fairy-woman began talking, and I heard every word they said, as no doubt they meant I should. 'What'll we do with the little beast at all?' says she.

"'We'll do something that's not too unpleasant at first,' says he. 'We'll take him and hold his head under the water, and see will that drive any of the devilment out of him.'

"'Oh, the thief!' says she. 'That's not the way to treat him at all. Let's heat the shovel and put him on it and throw him out the window.'

"'Ah, why will you be that cruel?' says he. 'Just let me heat the tongs red hot in the fire and then I'll catch him by the nose with them, and we'll find out will that make him go home and send poor Rickard back to us.'

"'That's not enough,' says she. 'I'll go and bring some of the juice of the lussmore that I have, and we'll make him drink it, and then if he's a fairy he'll wish that he was a man, so that he could die, it'll make that consternation inside him.'

"'We'll do the both of them things,' says he, and with that they both started into the kitchen, and all the rest of the people after them. But you may believe that by that time I was not there at all. I'd had enough of their kindness and I didn't think it was right to wait for any more of it. But I looked in at the window for a last glimpse of them, and one of the women saw me, and she screamed, and then the fairy-man made after me with the tongs, and I had to vanish completely. And you know what would happen then. When they drove me off, of course we had to send back Rickard, and there they found him the next morning, asleep in his bed, as sound as ever he was in his life.

"And that was not all. The lesson that he'd had was enough for him, and he left drinking and fighting and swearing, and he helped his old father and his brothers on the farm, and he was another man altogether. And so it's as I told you. You can never get the better of men, if they know anything, and all you do to hurt them only helps them. And so it will be if you send me to the Sullivans."

"If you're done talking about it now," said the King, "you'll go to the Sullivans and stay in the place of the child that we're to carry off. It's not likely they'll be leaving any pipes or any fiddle about for you to play on, and you can stay there quite comfortable.

"Off with him now!" the King cried to a dozen of his men, "and mind you don't come back without the child. And the same to you," he said again to others of his men; "take the woman and leave her in the place of the child at the O'Briens'."

The two parties were off, like two little swarms of bees, the one with Naggeneen and the other with the woman. The rest of the fairies waited. The Queen sat on her throne, with her face turned away from the rest and hidden in her hands. The King, with a troubled face, sat looking straight before him, not moving an eye or a hand. The others stood as far off as they could go. Nobody played; nobody danced; nobody laughed or whispered. They waited and watched and listened. Then there was a little murmur and buzz of one of the parties coming back. It was the one that had been to the Sullivans.

The King looked up and seemed to look through the fairies without seeing them. "Have you the child with you?" he asked.

"We have," said the leader.

"And where's Naggeneen?" the King asked.

"Lying in the bed beside Mrs. Sullivan," the leader answered, "and squealing like a pig under a gate."

"Give the child something to eat and make him comfortable," said the King.

The Queen turned suddenly around. "Don't give him anything to eat yet," she said. "We've nothing here but our own food. You couldn't give him that. What did you bring him here for? Was it not so that you could send him out again, as he grows up, to learn to do the things that men do? And if he touched a bit of our food or our drink, you know he could never leave us."

"That's the true word," said the King. "Here! Some of you go to the O'Briens' and see is there any milk left out of the window. And bring back enough so there'll be some for the other child, when we get her."

As the fairies set off on this errand there came a sound like the whistling of the wind through the door, and those who had gone to bring the O'Briens' child were back. They were back in a whirl and a rush and a scramble and a rout. They were all screaming and crying and whimpering and gabbling and gibbering together, and they all fell and sprawled together in a heap before the King. In the midst of them was the woman who had been sent to take the place of the O'Briens' child.

"What for are you here without the child?" the King cried. "And what are you all doing there on the floor, like fish tumbled out of a basket? Get up and tell me what's wrong with you! Where is the child?"

The fairies all choked and gasped and groaned and tried to speak. Then the leader of the party staggered up to his feet and stammered out: "The child is where it was before we went for it. We could not bring it; we could not take it; we could not touch it. You might as well be asking us to bring a lily from the fields of heaven."

"And why could you not take it?" the King asked. "Was the mother holding it so fast in her arms? Could you not make her look the other way while you'ld be taking it? Could you not put some charm on her so that she'ld let it go? Or was she praying all the time, so that you could do nothing with her? Or was she making those signs over it that none of us can stand?"

"No, no," said the leader, so low that they could scarcely hear him; "no, it wasn't that; the mother was doing none of them things. The mother was dead!"

For a minute everybody was still. The Queen started and looked at the leader of the party and leaned toward him. All the others gazed at him too. Then the King said, "And why did you not bring the child?"

"I'm after telling you we couldn't touch the child," the leader answered. "I went to take it, and all at once I felt burning hot, and like I was all dried up into a cinder, and I think they must have drawn a circle of fire round the child. And then I had that fearful feeling that you have when you're near a horseshoe nail. There must have been one somewhere about. You couldn't mistake that feeling — as if needles of ice were going all through and through you. And so I was driven back and could get no nearer to the child."

The woman who had been sent to take the place of the child was standing near the King now, though she could scarcely stand at all, and her face was all wet with tears. "But they made me go nearer to the child than that," she cried. "These others pushed me close to her, so that I'ld take her place and give the child to them. And I felt burned up like a cinder, too, and then I felt the icy needles, and then worse than that. I felt as if I was all cut across and across and through and through with flaming swords, and torn with red-hot saws. Not the way it is when you divide yourself, so that you can be in two places at once. Anybody can do that, and it hurts no more than cutting a lock of hair, but this was — oh! there's only one thing could do this. There was a pair of open scissors lying close to the child, and I almost touched them!"

She could say no more, and there was no more to be said. "You couldn't get the child, then," said the King, "and there's the end of it. Nobody could, if they did all them things. I dunno how it is," the King went on, half to himself, "a child lies there with a pair of scissors open near by, and a horseshoe nail close to it — maybe hung around its neck — and a circle drawn around it with a coal of fire, and it never minds it at all. It sleeps and wakes and lies there as peaceful and happy and quiet as if there was nothing at all out of the common about it. I dunno how they can do it. They're queer people, these mortals. We can't get the girl. They was too clever for us. But we've got the boy, and we'll do the best we can with him."

VI.
LITTLE KATHLEEN AND LITTLE TERENCE

The next morning John O'Brien was sitting alone, when there was a knock at the door. Then Peter Sullivan opened it, said "God save all here!" and came in.

"God save you kindly!" John answered.

"It's distressed we are," said Peter, "to hear of the death of poor Kitty. Ellen would be here with me to tell you so, only bein' in bed herself and not able to stir, and what'll come to all of us I dunno. I'm that disturbed about her I dunno what I'll do at all. I left her with one of the neighbors and came to see your mother about her. But sure it's you has the great grief on you already, whatever comes to us. It's not only you I'm thinkin' of, but it's the child, left with no mother. Oh, it's a terrible thing."

"My own mother can bring up any child," John answered. "Have no fear of that. It's us that knew Kitty that'll feel the loss of her."

"And how is the child doing, anyway?" Peter asked.

"She looks fine and healthy, glory be to God!" said John.

"It's a girl, they tell me."

"It is."

"Do you know yet what you'll call her?"

"We'll name her Kathleen, after her mother," said John.

"Then you'll be calling her Kitty, like her mother, I suppose."

"No — no," John answered, slowly; "I don't think I'll call her that. The child will be always Kathleen. I dunno if I can tell you how I feel about that. It was a name for a child, more than a woman — Kitty — and yet, now that she's gone from me, I've a feeling like it was something more than the name of a woman — like it was something holy, like the name of the blessed Mother of God. When I think of that name now, I want to think only of her, and I wouldn't like to be calling even her own child by it. It's Kathleen I'll call her — nothing else."

"You're right about all that, no doubt," said Peter; "but I can't be staying here, and Ellen and the child at home the way they are. You have your child left, and you say it's healthy — thank God for that same! — but it looks like I might have neither wife nor child."

"Don't say that, man alive," said John; "what's the matter at all then?"

"I can't stop discoursin' here," Peter answered. "I came to ask would your mother, being a knowledgable woman, step over for a bit and see can she tell at all what's the matter with Ellen and the child. There was a doctor there, but he seemed to do no good, and Ellen said your mother would know more than all the doctors, so I came to ask would she come. And if you care to come yourself, I'll be telling you how they are as we go along, but I can't stay here; it's too long to be away from them."

"Mother is with the child," said John; "I'll speak to her."

He went into another room, where the baby was sleeping and his mother was sitting beside her. He told her why Peter had come. "Step downstairs," said Mrs. O'Brien, "and ask Mrs. Mulvey will she sit by the baby till I'm back. Then I'll go with him. And you'd better come, too, John; the air will do you good."

John went down to another of the tenements in the house and came back with their neighbor, Mrs. Mulvey. "If you'll be so kind," Mrs. O'Brien said, "sit here by the baby till I'm back, and I'll not be long. And mind you keep everything as it is, unless she wakes, and then you'll know what to do as well as I, for you've children of your own. But don't disturb the pair of scissors that's there beside her, and don't take off the horseshoe nail that's hung round her neck."

"And what's them things for?" Mrs. Mulvey asked, with wonder in her eyes.

"Why, to keep the Good People from stealing the child," Mrs. O'Brien answered. "Did you never hear of those things? Don't you know the Good People can't stand the touch of iron, or even to be near it? And especially a horseshoe nail they can't stand. And the scissors, too, they couldn't come near, and then leaving them open they make a cross, and that keeps the child all the more from the Good People."

John and his mother left Mrs. Mulvey with little Kathleen and went with Peter. "And what's wrong with Ellen, then?" Mrs. O'Brien asked.

"I dunno that there's so much wrong with herself, as you might say," Peter answered. "I think it's more than anything else that she's worried about the child."

"And what's wrong with the child, then?"

"There's everything wrong with the child," said Peter. "It's not like the same child at all. Last night he was as healthy a boy as you'ld wish to see — quiet and peaceable and good-tempered and strong-looking, for his age. And now this morning he's thin and sick-looking, and there's black hair all over his arms, and his face is wrinkled, like he was a little old man, and he does nothing but cry and scream till you can't bear it, and twist and squirm till you can't hold him. It's like he was fairy-struck, only I don't believe in them things at all."

"Did you watch him close last night?" Mrs. O'Brien asked.

"Part of the time," Peter answered, "but I dare say we was both asleep other times."

"Was Ellen careful about her prayers last night, and were you so, too?"

"I can't say about that," Peter said. "We might be letting some of them go, such a time as that, you know, and make it up after."

"Yes," said Mrs. O'Brien, "make it up after by losing your child! Was there any iron anywhere about him?"

"I don't know that there was."

"And did you make a circle of fire about the place where he was lying?"

"I did not."

"The child's not been struck," said Mrs. O'Brien; "not the way you mean. It's not your child at all, but one of the Good People themselves, that's in it. They've stolen your child and left a changeling in the place of it."

"It's the same way you always talked, Mrs. O'Brien," said Peter. "I don't believe them things."

They had come to Peter's door by this time. They found Ellen lying in bed, looking frightened half to death, and beside her was the baby, or the fairy, or whatever it was. It was not crying loudly now, but it was keeping up a little whining and whimpering noise that was quite as unpleasant to listen to as a good, honest cry. Its face looked thin and pinched and old; it had a little thin, wispy hair on its head where no baby of the age that this one was supposed to be has a right to have any. Its arms and hands were thin and bony. It looked weak and sick, but it was rolling and wriggling about in the liveliest way. It would give a spring as if it were going straight off the bed upon the floor, and when poor Ellen caught at it to save it, it would roll back toward her, stop its crying for a second, and seem to be laughing at her, and then it would do the same thing again.

"It's plain enough," Mrs. O'Brien said, as soon as she saw it. "It's one of the Good People. But it's quick enough we'll be rid of it and have back your own child. Bring me some eggs."

"I'll have nothing of the sort now," said Ellen. "It's bad the poor child is with some sickness or other, but it's my own child, and I'll have nothing done to it that's not to do it good. If you know anything that'll help it, Mrs. O'Brien, tell me that, but don't be sayin' it's not my child."

"I'll not hurt the child, whatever it is," said Mrs. O'Brien, "but there are ways to tell whether it's your own child at all or one of the Good People. If you find it's one of them, then it's easy to do more, but in the meantime it's not harmed."

"I'll not have you trying any of them things," said Ellen. "I'll not have you saying it's not my child, and I'll not be thinking of such a thing myself. You see how poor and sick it's looking. If there's anything you can do for the child, do it, but don't be talking that way any more."

"Ellen," said Mrs. O'Brien, "you don't know what you're talking about at all. Wait now till I tell you what was told to me when I lived in Dublin, and I think that it was not far from there that it happened. It's about a woman that talked as you do. A sailor's wife she was, and there was a child born to her while her husband was away at sea. She thought he'ld be home soon, and so she wanted to put off the christening of the child till he'ld be back. So she waited and waited for a long time, and her husband did not come. The neighbors told her she was doing wrong to wait so long and she ought to have the child christened before anything would happen to it. But she wouldn't listen to them.

"So it went on for a year and a half, and still the father didn't come home. But the boy was healthy and happy, and the mother never had any trouble with him. But the trouble came. One day she'd been working in the field, and she came home, and as soon as she was in the house she heard crying from the bed where the child used to sleep. She ran to look at him, and he lay there, looking sick and thin and weak, the way your boy does, and crying that he was hungry. He was like her child and he was not like him. He'd grown so pale and bad-looking that she thought he'd had a stroke from the Good People. But she went to get him some bread and milk, and she asked her other boy, that was about seven years old, when it was and how it was that he began to be sick.

"'I left him playing near the fire,' the boy said, 'and I was in the other room. And I heard a rushing noise, like a great flock of birds flying down the chimney, and then I heard a cry from my brother and then again the noise, like the birds were flying out at the chimney again. And then I ran in and found him there the way you see him now.'

"Well, if the poor woman had never had trouble with the child before, she had nothing but trouble now. Crying and squalling it was all the time, and it nearly ate her out of house and home, and yet it seemed always sick and weak and thin. The neighbors came and they told her it was not her child at all, but one of the Good People that had been put in the place of it, and it was all her own fault for not having it christened in the right time. But not a word of it all would she listen to, and she said all the time that, whatever was wrong with it, it was her own child and she'ld hear nothing to the contrary.

"It was an out-of-the-way place where they lived, and there was no priest near, or she never could have kept it from being christened as long as she did. But at last the neighbors themselves said that if she didn't see to it, they would. And they said to her: 'It's not your child at all that's in it, and if you'll have it christened you'll see. And if you won't take the child to the priest with us now, we'll go to him ourselves and tell him all about it. It's not right to keep it from him longer.'

"So with that she thought it was no use and she'ld have to do as they said, and she took the child and tried to dress him, ready to take him to the priest to be christened. But the roars and the screams that he let out of him were more than anybody could bear, and at the last she said: 'Oh, I can't do it; it's too terrible a thing for him; he won't bear it, and how can I make him?'

"The next day when she came in from her work the other boy said to her: 'Mother, it was uncommon quiet he was while you was away to-day. And by and by I went in to see what was ailing him. And there he sat, looking so like an old man that I was near afraid of him. And he looked at me and he spoke as plain as an old man, and he says: "Pat," says he, "bring me a pipe, till I have a bit of a smoke. It's tired of life I am, lying here without it."'

"'"Ah," says I, "wait till my mother gets home and I'll tell her of this."'

"'"Tell her," says he, "and she'll not believe a word from you."'

"'And no more do I believe a word from you,' says the woman.

"Well, soon after that there came a letter from the father, saying that he'ld be at home now in a few days. With that the woman set off to town to buy things to eat and drink to welcome her husband home, and she said: 'Now we'll have the christening, as soon as ever he comes.'

"Then as soon as she was off, the neighbors said: 'Now is the time that we'll be done with that imp. We'll take him and have him christened while she's away, and we'll not give her the chance to put it off again because he cries.'

"PLUMP DOWN HE FELL THROUGH THE QUILT."

"So they went to the house and one of the women came up to the bed and clapped a quilt over him and had him wrapped up in it before he knew what was happening to him, and away they all went down toward the brook, on the way to the priest. Well, he kicked and he struggled to get free, but the woman held him so tight it was no use. But when they came to the running water, it

95

was then he began bellowing like a herd of bulls, and kicking and pulling so that it was all she could do to hold him.

"She got her foot on the first of the stepping-stones, and it was then he began to get heavy, as if it was a stone that she was carrying. But she held hard and reached the second stone, and it seemed to her that he was nothing but a lump of lead, only still roaring and struggling; and, what with that and the rushing of the water below her, she began to get dizzy, but still she held on, and she had her foot on the stone in the middle of the stream when plump down he fell through the quilt that he was wrapped in, as if it had been nothing but a muslin handkerchief.

"And there he went floating down the stream, and shouting and laughing at them. For, you know, it's not being in running water that can hurt one of the Good People, but only crossing it, and if they tried to cross it they'ld be in awful pain till they got to the middle, and then nothing could keep them from falling in.

"So they were rid of him, and you know when you're rid of a changeling the Good People must send your own child back. And so the neighbors had not got back to the house when they met the mother running to meet them and bringing her own child, that she had found in its bed, when she got back from the town, sleeping, as well and as sound as ever it was.

"And now, Ellen," said Mrs. O'Brien, "will you let me try, in ways that I know, that can do no harm, whether this is your own child or not? And if it's not, you'll have your own back, as well as it was last night."

"This is my own child," Ellen answered, "and it's not by any silly tales like that that you can make me believe it isn't. I'll not have you doing anything of the sort. If you know anything that can help a baby when it's sick, you may do that, but nothing else."

"I do know one thing that can help a sick baby," Mrs. O'Brien answered "and that I'll do, if you like it or not. If that thing there is one of the Good People, as I think, it's not sick, and it will live for thousands of years after we are dead. We can neither help it nor much hurt it. But if that is your child, it doesn't look to me as if it would live an hour. I'll not try whether it's yours or not, but if it's yours I'll not stand by and see its soul die, that ought to be the soul of a Christian. Ellen Sullivan, that child will be christened before I leave this house."

"Christened!" poor Ellen cried in amazement. "And who's to christen him? We couldn't get a priest here in an hour — maybe not to-day."

"There's no need of a priest," Mrs. O'Brien said; "I'll christen him myself. Bring me some water there, Peter."

"But sure you can't do that," Peter protested. "Nobody but a priest could christen a child."

"I can christen the child as well as a priest," said Mrs. O'Brien; "you take a child to the priest to be christened, when it's easy and convenient, but when there's no priest near, and the child is sick and seems likely to die before one can come, anybody can christen it; and that christening stands, and it never has to be christened after. That's the law of the Church. Bring me the water. I never saw a child that seemed more likely to die than this one, if it's a child at all."

And Peter brought the water.

"What do you call the child?" Mrs. O'Brien asked.

"I think we'll call him Terence," Peter answered. "That was my grandfather's name, on my mother's side, and a decent man he was, and uncommon fond of myself when I was a bit of a gossoon, till he died, Heaven rest his soul! and I think I'd like to name the boy after him."

Now all that the child had been doing and all the noise that he had been making before were simply nothing to what he had been doing ever since Mrs. O'Brien first said the word "christen." He was screaming so that all this talk could scarcely be heard, and it was almost more than Mrs. O'Brien could do to hold him, when she took him in her arms. But she did hold him for a moment with one arm, while she dipped up some water with her hand and sprinkled it over him. Then the creature gave one great jump and was away from her and fell on the floor.

Before anybody else could move, Mrs. O'Brien herself picked him up and laid him on the bed. There was no sign that he was hurt. No child that was hurt could have screamed as he did. "Come, John," said Mrs. O'Brien, "we've done all that we can."

"May I walk back with you a piece?" said Peter. "There was something more that I was thinking I would say."

"Come back with us, of course, and welcome," said John.

They left the house and walked along the street.

"I think it was right, what you done, Mrs. O'Brien," said Peter. "I can't think about the child the way you think, but it was right what you done."

Mrs. O'Brien made no answer. "John," said Peter, "there's something that I was thinking of last night and this morning, and it was this: You have a girl and I have a boy, that was both born on the one day. It's good friends we've always been, and your father and your mother and my father and my mother before us. And I was just thinking when your girl and my boy grows up, supposing that they like each other well enough, it might be pleasant to all of us that they'ld be married some time.

"There's no man's son that I'd rather see a daughter of mine married to than yours, Peter," said John, "if she herself was pleased. I'ld not ask her to take anybody she didn't like, but if she came to love him, and he came to love her, I'ld be as pleased as yourself."

"It was that I wanted to say," said Peter, "and I'd better go back to Ellen now."

John and his mother said no more till they were at home. They both went into the room where little Kathleen was. Mrs. Mulvey sat watching the baby. She went out and left them. The child was sleeping as peacefully as if there were no such thing in the world as sorrow or loss or doubt, or a fairy to help or harm.

"John," said Mrs. O'Brien, "I'd think I might have done harm to that child in trying to christen it, only I'm as sure as ever I was of anything that it's not a child at all, but one of the Good People, so I think there's no harm done. I don't know what would happen any of the Good People if he was to be rightly christened. I think he'ld not be able to stand it and would be driven out, so that they'ld have to send back the real child. Now, if a priest ever sees that creature that we've just seen, and asks: 'Has this child been christened?' they'll have to answer 'Yes,' and he cannot be christened again. And yet, with the jump that he gave out of my arms when I sprinkled the water, it's not sure I am that a drop of it touched him."

VII.
A CHAPTER THAT YOU CAN SKIP

This is a chapter that you can skip, if you want to. And really I should advise you to. Nothing of importance happened in the next eighteen years. Of course I am obliged to write a little something to fill in all that time, but you are not obliged to read it. That is where you have such an advantage. I think it is much better for a book to have some parts that can be skipped just as well as not, you get through it so much faster. I have often thought what a good thing it would be if somebody would write a book that we could skip the whole of. I think a good many people would like to have such a book as that. I know I should.

Then there is another reason why it will be well for you to skip a little about here. When you get farther on, if you happen to come to something that you don't understand, you can say: "Oh, this is probably all explained by something in that part that I skipped," and you can go right on. But if you had not skipped anything and then came to something that you did not understand, you would have to say: "There, now, I must have been reading carelessly and missed something," and you would have to go back and read the book all through again.

In these eighteen years Kathleen O'Brien and Terence Sullivan were growing up. I don't suppose there ever was another such child as Kathleen. And I should hope there never was another such child as Terence. Kathleen's grandmother had the most of the care of her, of course, but it was really no care at all. It would have been a pleasure for anybody to have the care of Kathleen. Even when she was a baby she was a perfect delight, and you know what babies are sometimes. At any rate, you would know, if you had known Terence. And when she got to be a few years older, say seven or eight —

Well, it is perfectly impossible for me to tell you how good and lovely Kathleen was. It is all very well to try to describe snow-capped mountains at sunrise, or a storm at sea, or moonlight at Niagara, or a prairie on fire, or anything of that sort, but nobody could tell you how good and lovely Kathleen was, so that you could understand it. I suppose she was a good deal the sort of child that you would be if you didn't put your elbows on the table, or your spoon in your mouth, or slam the doors, or cry when your hair is combed, or tease for things that you ought not to have, or whisper in company, or talk out loud when there are older persons present, or leave your playthings about when you are done with them, or get your clothes soiled when you play out of doors, or want to play at all when you ought to study your lessons, or ask to be allowed to sit up after bed-time, or bite your nails, or cut your bread, or leave your spoon in your cup instead of in your saucer, or take the biggest apple.

I don't say that Kathleen never did any of these things. I only say that she was so good that you would have to leave off every one of them or you would never catch up with her. If Kathleen had a fault, it was that she was too good. If I were going to have anything to do with her I would rather she should be a little bit worse than a single bit better. I am so glad you are skipping this part, because I shouldn't want you to try to be a bit worse than you are just for the sake of pleasing me. And I don't mean by all this that Kathleen was one of those children who are a bother all the time because they are so good. She may have done things that she ought not to do sometimes. I dare say she did. I know she did once. I will tell you all about that in the next chapter. She was just a dear, sweet little girl, as bright and merry and healthy as any little girl in the world ever was. And you would think so yourself, if you had known her and were not so jealous. If I should tell you that she was as pretty as she was good, I don't suppose you would believe me. But she was, just as surely as I am writing this book and you are reading it. I mean just as surely as I am writing it. I am not sure yet whether you are reading it or not.

But Terence! Well, the less said about him the better. Still, I suppose, I shall have to say something. He did every one of the things that I have just mentioned. And it wasn't because he didn't know any better; he seemed to like to do them, just because he knew that they were wrong. When he was a baby he was more trouble than twins, and bad twins at that. He cried all the time, except when he was eating or sleeping, and he slept only a little of the time and ate a great deal of it. He always seemed to be just about so sick, but it never hurt his appetite and he never got any sicker. After a while Ellen got used to his being sick, and she always said that he was delicate, poor child, and that was why he was so cross and so much trouble.

"And is that why he eats so much?" Mrs. O'Brien would ask.

"I dunno about that," Ellen would answer; "I think it's the kind of sickness that's on him that makes him eat so much."

"More likely it's eating so much that gives him the kind of sickness that's on him," Mrs. O'Brien would say. "But I tell you again, it's no sickness at all he has. He s just one of the Good People, and you could be rid of him and have your own child back any time you would do any of the things I would tell you."

But not a word of this would Ellen ever heed. Terence was her own child, and he might be a bit troublesome, as any child might, but he was not really bad at all, and it was Kathleen, that was always so good, the Lord knew why, that made Mrs. O'Brien think that every child ought to be that way. But there was one strange thing about Terence, and Ellen herself had to admit it. After that very hour, when he was one day old, when Mrs. O'Brien came to see him and christened him, or tried to — she never felt sure till long afterward whether she had done it or not — he was always quiet when she was near. He would drive poor Ellen nearly crazy, in spite of all her excuses for him, when he was alone with her, but the moment that Mrs. O'Brien came into the house he would get as far away from her as he could, and then lie perfectly still and watch her, for all the world, as John said once, like a rat in a trap watching a cat. Ellen said that it was because he always remembered that it was Mrs. O'Brien who had dropped him once. To this John replied: "Then maybe he'ld be making you less trouble, Ellen, if you was to drop him yourself once or twice." But Mrs. O'Brien said that it was just because he knew what she would do to him if she had the chance.

And there was another strange thing about Terence. As he grew a little older, he never could be got inside a church. Father Duffy had never even seen him, except when he came to the house while he was still a baby, and then Terence would scream and kick so, when the good priest came near him, that he never dared touch him. The first time that he came, Ellen told him about Mrs. O'Brien's christening the child, and asked him if it was right for her to do it.

"Was the child looking sick, and as if he was likely to die?" Father Duffy asked.

"He was, father," Ellen answered; "I couldn't deny that."

"Then it was right for her to christen him," the priest answered, "and he'll not need to be christened again. In fact, he can't be christened again."

But long after that, when they tried to take him to church, he would never go. If Peter and Ellen started for church with him he would run away from them. They could not even hold him. He would get away from them, and sometimes they could not tell how he did it, only he would be gone. And then the only way that they could find him was to go home again, and there he was sure to be, as safe as ever, only he had not been at church. And so, after a while, they stopped trying to make him go.

When the two children were old enough to play together, Terence never seemed to be happy except when he was with Kathleen. He did not care in the least to play with other boys. He did not seem to care in the least to play at all. All he wanted was to be with Kathleen. Kathleen never liked him, and she did not like to have him with her so much of the time. But she was too kind-hearted to hurt anybody in any way, even a boy whom she did not like, so she tried to treat him as nicely as she could, and she told nobody but her grandmother, to whom she told everything, that she was not as pleased to be with him as he was to be with her.

Terence, in his turn, did not always treat Kathleen well, any more than he did anybody else. He was ill-natured with her and he played tricks on her that were not pleasant at all, and yet he wanted to be always with her. Perhaps it was partly because she was more kind to him than anybody else, except Ellen. For nobody else liked him. And if he was bad-tempered and unkind to other people, it made other people unkind and bad-tempered to him, but nothing could make Kathleen unkind to anybody.

"It's not fair you all are to Terence," Ellen said once to Mrs. O'Brien, "to think bad of him the way you do. There's things about him that don't seem right, I know, but those things don't show the way he really is. I dunno if I'm making you understand me. I'm his mother and I know him better nor anybody else, and I know he's different from the way he seems to you, and even the way he seems to me sometimes. And I'll tell you how I know that. When I'm asleep I often dream about him. And when I dream about him, he looks a little the way he does other times, but he's taller and he's better-looking in the face, and he looks stronger and brighter and healthier like. And he speaks to me, and his voice is lower and pleasanter in the sound of it. And that's the way he'ld be, I know, if he had his health, poor child, and if everything was right with him. And you'ld all know that and you'ld feel more for him, if you knew him the way I do."

This was when Terence was six or seven years old. And Ellen often spoke in this way afterward. She saw Terence in her dreams, and he was a very different Terence from the one who made her so much trouble when she was awake, and yet he was partly the same.

And there was one thing that Terence did that almost everybody liked. I might as well say everybody except Kathleen. He played the fiddle. Nobody knew how he learned. There was a neighbor of the Sullivans who came from the same county in Ireland that they did, and he played a fiddle in an orchestra at a cheap theatre. One day Peter had gone to see this man and had taken little Terence with him. The fiddle was lying on the table. The two men went into another room and left Terence by himself. They were talking busily and they forgot about him. Then they heard a soft little tune played on the fiddle. "Who's that playing my fiddle?" said the owner of it.

"Sure," said Peter, 'we left nobody there but Terence."

They went quickly back into the room and found Terence hastily laying the fiddle down where he had found it. "Ah, can't I leave you alone a minute," said Peter, "but you must be meddling with things that don't belong to you? What'll I do now if you've gone and hurt the fiddle?"

"Don't be talking that way to the child," said the musician; "sure he did it no harm. But where at all did he learn to play that way? That's what I'm thinking. Have you been letting him learn all this time and never told me?"

"He never learned at all that I know of," Peter answered. "I never saw him have a fiddle in his hand till this minute."

"It's a strange thing, then," the musician said. "Anybody that can play a tune like he did that one has a right to play more and better. Where did you learn it, my boy?"

"I never learned it at all," Terence answered; "I just saw the fiddle there and I thought I'ld see could I play it. But it's little I could be doing with it, I'm thinking."

Peter was surprised enough to find that Terence could play a tune on a fiddle, and so was Ellen, when she heard about it. But they did not wonder at it so much as they would have done if they had known more about such things. They had a sort of notion that one person could play the fiddle and another could not, much as one person can move his ears and another cannot. So they thought little about it. But when Terence begged them to buy him a fiddle of his own, they saved up money a little at a time, and at last they bought him one.

Then for days Terence did nothing but play. He played simple little tunes at first, but soon he began to play harder ones. Then he got impatient with himself, as it seemed, and he began to play such music as nobody who heard him had ever heard before. Often he would not play when he was asked, but he would play for hours by himself, when he thought that no one was listening. His father brought his friend the musician to hear him, and he said that it was wonderful. He had never heard the fiddle played so well. Nobody had ever heard the fiddle played so well.

And Kathleen never cared to hear Terence play. She did hear him play, many times, of course, and she listened politely, but she told her grandmother that she did not care about it at all. She would much rather hear the poor fiddler of the little orchestra, who had come from their county in Ireland. Their neighbor the fiddler himself was as much shocked as anyone to hear Kathleen talk like this. "Did you ever hear anybody play the fiddle like Terence plays it?" he asked her, when she said something of the sort to him.

"No," Kathleen answered. "I never heard anybody play it like Terence, but I have heard some play it better than Terence. You play it better."

"Oh, child," he said, "I'ld give all the money I'll be earning in the next ten years if I could play like he does. Don't you see I can't do half the things he does with it?"

"I know that," Kathleen said; "it isn't the way he plays a bit that makes everybody talk so about him; it's just the things he does. When he plays a tune it just doesn't mean anything, and when you play a tune it does."

And that was as near as Kathleen could ever come to telling why she did not care about Terence's playing. Everybody else said that it was wonderful, but she said that it didn't mean anything. And when Kathleen talked in this way they said that she was too critical. That is what people will always tell you when you can see through a fraud and they cannot.

You will suppose, without my telling you, that as soon as Kathleen was old enough to listen to them, her grandmother began telling her the old stories of Ireland. Often Terence would come and listen to them, too, for he seemed to be less afraid of Mrs. O'Brien as he grew a little older. But it never seemed to be because of the stories that he came; he only wanted to be near Kathleen.

Mrs. O'Brien told the children stories about the Good People, and about the old heroes and kings of Ireland who had fought to save the country from its enemies. Terence never liked the stories about the Good People. "Don't be telling us about them fairies all the time," he would say. "Tell us about men; that's what I like better."

"Don't call them by that name," Mrs. O'Brien would answer. "They don't like it, and if you call them by it they may do you harm."

"I'll call them what I like," Terence would say, "and they'll do me no harm. It's a worthless lot they are, and you know that same yourself, Mrs. O'Brien, if you'ld only think so. They can do no harm to you, or to any woman or man that knows how to deal with them. Why will you bother with them all the time?"

And all this made Mrs. O'Brien think the more that Terence was one of them.

One day Mrs. O'Brien happened to tell the children a ghost story. I don't know whether your mother allows you to read ghost stories. I don't see any harm in them myself, any more than Mrs. O'Brien did, but some people do, and if your mother does, then it is lucky that you are skipping this part. I think that your mother will be very glad that you skipped this part with the ghost story in it. That is, of course, she won't really be glad, because, since you are skipping it, you won't know that there is any ghost story here, and so you won't tell your mother that you skipped a ghost story, and so she won't really care whether you skipped it or not. What I mean is that if you had read it instead of skipping it, so that you could tell your mother that there was a ghost story, she would be glad that you had skipped — well, what is the use of my trying to tell you what I mean, as long as you are skipping it, anyway? I had better go on with the story.

"Once a man was coming home from a funeral," said Mrs. O'Brien. "As he was walking along the road, near a churchyard, he found the head of a man. He took it up and left it in the churchyard. Then he went on his way, and soon he met a man who looked like a gentleman.

"'Where have you been?' said the gentleman.

"'I was at a funeral,' said the man, 'and as I came back I found the head of a man, and I left it in the churchyard.'

"'It was well for you that you did that,' said the gentleman. 'That was my head, and if you had done any wrong by it, it would be the worse for you.'

"'And how did you lose your head, then?' the man asked.

"'I did not lose it,' the gentleman answered; 'I left it on the road, where you found it, to see what you would do with it.'

"'Then you must be one of the Good People,' said the man, 'and it's sorry I am that I met you.'

"'Don't be afraid,' said the gentleman. 'I'll do you no harm, and I may do you good.'

"'I'm obliged to you,' said the man; 'will you come home with me to dinner?'

"They went to the man's house, and the man told his wife to get dinner ready for them. When they had eaten dinner they played cards, and then they went to bed and slept till morning. In the morning they had breakfast, and after a while the gentleman said: 'Come with me.'

"'Where am I to come with you?' the man asked.

"'I want you to see the place where I live,' the gentleman said.

"They went together till they came to the churchyard. The gentleman pointed to a tombstone and said: 'Lift it up.'

"The man lifted it up, and there was a stairway underneath. They went down the stairs together till they came to a door, and it led into a kitchen. Two women were sitting by the fire. Said the gentleman to one of the women: 'Get up and get dinner ready for us.'

"The woman got up and brought some small potatoes. 'Are those all you have for us?' the gentleman asked.

"'Those are all I have,' the woman answered.

"'As those are all you have,' said the gentleman, 'keep them.'

"Then he said to the other woman: 'Get up and get dinner ready for us.'

"The woman got up and brought some meal and husks. 'Are those all you have?' the gentleman asked.

"'Those are all I have,' the woman answered.

"'As those are all you have,' said the gentleman, 'keep them.'

"He led the man up the stairs and knocked at a door. A beautiful woman opened it. She was dressed in a gown of silk, and it was all trimmed with gold and jewels. He asked her if she could give him and the stranger a dinner. Then she placed before them the finest dinner that was ever seen. And when they had eaten and drunk as much as they liked, the gentleman said: 'Do you know why this woman was able to give us such a dinner?'

"'I do not know,' said the man, 'but I should like to know, if you care to tell me.'

"'When I was alive,' said the gentleman, 'I had three wives. And the first wife I had would never give anything to any poor man but little potatoes. And now she has nothing but little potatoes herself, and she can give nothing else to anyone, till the Day of Judgment. And my second wife would never give anything to the poor but meal and husks, and now she has nothing but meal and husks herself, and she can give nothing else to anyone, till the Day of Judgment. But my third wife always gave to the poor the best that she had, and so she will always have the best that there is in the world, and she can always give the best in the world to anyone, till the Day of Judgment.'

"Then the gentleman took the man about and showed him his house, and it was a palace, more beautiful than anything that he had ever seen. And while he was walking about it he heard music. And he thought that he had never heard music so beautiful. And while he was listening to the music he felt like sleeping, so he lay down and slept. And when he woke he was in his own home. He never saw the gentleman again and he could never find the place where he had been."

"It's all the time fairies and ghosts with you, Mrs. O'Brien," Terence said. "Who cares what they do? It's what men do that counts. I'll tell you a story now."

So Mrs. O'Brien and Kathleen listened to Terence's story.

"There was three men," Terence began, "that lived near together, and their names was Hudden and Dudden and Donald. Each one of them had an ox that he'ld be ploughing with. Donald was a cleverer man than the others and he got on better. So the other two put their heads together to think what would they do to hurt Donald and to ruin him entirely, so that he'ld have to give up his farm and they could get it cheap. Well, after a while they thought that if they could kill his ox he couldn't plough his land, and then he'ld lose the use of it and he'ld have to give it up. So one night they went and killed Donald's ox.

"And to be sure, when Donald found his ox killed, he thought it was all over with him. But he wasn't the man to be thinking that way long. So he thought he'd better make the best he could of it, and he took the skin off the ox and started with it to the town to sell it. And as he was going along a magpie perched on the skin and began pecking at it, and all the time chattering, for it had been taught to talk. With that Donald put round his hand and caught the magpie and held it under his coat.

"He went on to the town and sold the skin, and then he went to an inn for a drink. He followed the landlady down into the cellar, and while she was drawing the liquor he pinched the magpie and it began chattering again. 'By the powers,' says the landlady, 'who's that talking and what's he saying at all?'

"'It's a bird,' says Donald, 'that I carry around with me, and it knows a great deal and tells me many a thing that it's good for me to know. And it's after telling me just now that the liquor you're giving me is not the best you have.'

"'It's the wonderful bird all out,' says the landlady, and with that she went to another cask for the liquor. Then said she: 'Will you sell that bird?'

"'I wouldn't like to do that,' says Donald. 'It's a valuable bird, and then it's been my friend a long time, and I dunno what it would be thinking of me if I'd sell it.'

"'Maybe I'ld make it worth your while.' said the landlady.

"'I'm a poor man,' says Donald.

"'I'll fill your hat with silver,' says the landlady, 'if you'll leave me the bird.'

"'I couldn't refuse that,' says Donald; 'you may have the bird.'

"So she filled his hat with silver, and he left her the bird and went on his way home.

"It wasn't long after he got home till he met Hudden and Dudden. 'Aha!' says he to them, 'you thought it was the bad turn you was doing me, but you couldn't have done me a better. Look what I got for the hide of my ox, that you killed on me.' And he showed them the hatful of silver. 'You never saw such a demand for hides in your life,' says he, 'as there is in the town this present time.'

"No sooner had he said that than Hudden and Dudden went home and killed their own oxen and set off for the town to sell the hides. But when they got there they could get no more for them than the common price of hides, and they came home again vowing vengeance on Donald.

"This time they were bound there would be no mistake about it, so they went to his house and they seized him and put him into a sack and tied up the top of it. 'Now,' says one of them, 'you'll not be doing us any dirty turn this time, I'm thinking. We're going to take you to the river and throw you in and drown you; that's what we're going to do and I'm telling you of it now, so that you'll have the pleasure of thinking that all your sorrows are nearly over, as you go along.'

"Well, Donald said never a word, but he kept thinking, and those words 'all your sorrows are nearly over' gave him something particular to think about, and it wasn't long till he began to see his way, if he could only get a chance to do what he was thinking of.

"THERE'S A BLESSING ON THIS SAME SACK.'

"They took up the sack and they carried it by turns for a time, but both of them soon began to get mighty tired and thirsty. Then they came to a tavern, and they left the sack outside, and Donald in it, and went in to get a drink. Donald knew that if they once began drinking they would stay inside for some time. Then presently he heard a great trampling sound, and he knew it must be a herd of cattle coming, and he knew there must be somebody driving them. With that he began singing, like he was the happiest man in the world.

"The man that was driving the cattle came up to him and he says: 'Who's inside the sack there, and what are you singing like that for?'

"'I'm singing because I'm the happiest man alive,' says Donald. 'I had plenty of troubles in my life, but I'm going to heaven now, and they're all over. There's a blessing on this same sack, you must know, and whoever's in it goes straight to heaven, and isn't it myself that's a right to be singing?'

"'Surely you have,' says the man, 'and it's glad I'ld be to take your place. What would you take from me now to let me get in that sack in your place?'

"'There's not money enough in the world to make me do it,' says Donald, and he began singing again.

"'Ah, be reasonable!' says the man. 'I'll pay you well.'

"'I tell you the whole world couldn't do it,' says Donald. 'It's not every day a man gets a chance to go to heaven. Think of being over with all the sorrows and the troubles of this world, and nothing but happiness any more forever. Sure I'ld be a fool if I'ld give it up.'

"'Oh, but think of me,' says the man. 'It's me that has the sorrows on me so that I can't bear them. There's my wife died three months ago, and all the children was dead before her, and it was she always helped me with the farm and knew how to manage better nor myself, so that now she's gone I can do nothing with it. And I've lost money on it till I can't pay the rent, and now I'll lose the farm itself, and here I am driving these cattle to town to sell them to get money to take another piece of land and keep the life in me, and yet I don't want to live at all. Oh, give me your place in that sack and you'll go to heaven in your own time, if it was only for that one good deed. Give me your place and I'll give you these twenty fine cattle, and you'll have better luck nor me and you'll surely do well with them.'

"'I can't resist you,' says Donald; 'sure it's you needs to go to heaven more nor me. It's the truth I hate to do it, but I'll give you my place.'

"So with that the man untied the sack and Donald got out of it and he got into it, and Donald tied it up again. Then Donald went away home, driving the cattle before him.

"It was not long then till Hudden and Dudden came out of the inn, and they took up the sack, thinking that Donald was still inside it, and they took it to the river and threw it into a deep place. Then they went home, and there they found Donald before them, and a herd of the finest cattle they ever saw. 'How is this, Donald?' they said. 'We drowned you in the river, and here you are back home before us. And where are you after getting all these cattle?'

"'Oh, sure,' says Donald, 'it's myself has the bad luck all out. Here I've only twenty of these cattle, and if I'd only had help I could have had a hundred — aye, or five hundred. Sure in the place where you threw me in, down at the bottom of the river, there was hundreds of the finest cattle you ever saw, and plenty of gold besides. Oh, it's the misfortunate creature that I am, not to have any help while I was down there. Just these poor twenty was all I could manage to drive away with me, and these not the best that was there.'

"Then they both swore that they would be his friends if he would only show them the place in the river where they could get cattle like his. So he said he'ld show them the place and they could drive home as many of them as they liked. Well, Hudden and Dudden was in such a hurry they couldn't get to the river soon enough, and when they were there Donald picked up a stone, and said he: 'Watch where I throw this stone, and that's where you'll find the most of the cattle.'

"Then he threw the stone into a deep part of the river, and he said: 'One of you jump in there now, and if you find more of the cattle than you can manage, just come to the top and call for help, and the other two of us will come in and help you.'

"So Hudden jumped in first and he went straight to the bottom. In a minute he came up to the top and shouted: 'Help! help '

"'He's calling for help,' says Donald; 'wait now till I go in and help him.'

"'Stay where you are,' says Dudden; 'haven't you cattle enough already? It's my turn to have some of them now.' And in he jumped, and Hudden and Dudden was both drowned. And then Donald went home and looked after his cattle and his farm, and soon he made money enough to take the two farms that Hudden and Dudden had left, besides his own.

"And that's the way," said Terence, "to get on in this world or any world. Get the better of them that's trying to get the better of you, and don't hope for any help from fairies or ghosts."

"Terence," said Mrs. O'Brien, "there's a little that's right in what you say, and there's more that's wrong. Depend on yourself and don't look for help from Good People or ghosts. So much of what you say is right. But Donald was not honest and he got on by tricks, and I don't want you or Kathleen to be that way. You'll not get on that way; you'll only come to grief. But I want you to be kind and helpful to mortals and Good People because it's right to be so, not to get any reward. The reward you may get or you may not in this world, but it's not that I want you to work for. And I'll tell you a story now to show you what I mean.

"There was a poor little bit of a boy once, and he had a hump on his back. He made his living by plaiting rushes and straw into hats and baskets and beehives, and he could do it better than anybody else for miles around. I don't know what his right name was, but the people called him Lusmore, after the flower of that name. The flower, you know, is the one that some call fairy-cap — the Lord between us and harm! — and others call it foxglove. And they called him after it, because he would always be wearing a sprig of it in his cap. And in spite of having a crooked back, which often makes a body sulky, he was a good-natured little fellow, and never had a bad word or a bad thought for anybody.

"One day he had been at a fair to sell some of the things that he made out of straw and rushes, and as he was coming home he felt tired with the long walk. So he sat down to rest for a little, and he leaned his back on a bank of earth, not thinking that it was a place that was said to be a rath of the Good People. He sat there for a long time, and at last he began to hear music. It was very soft at first, and he had to listen hard to catch it at all. Then it sounded clearer, and after a little he could tell that there were

115

fiddlers and pipers. Then he thought that he could hear the feet of dancers, and finally singers, and he could hear the words of the song that they sang. And these were the words:

Da Luan, da Mort,
Da Luan, da Mort,
Da Luan, da Mort.

"And there were no other words but these, and these the singers sang over and over and over again. And all they mean is, 'Monday, Tuesday, Monday, Tuesday, Monday, Tuesday.' After the singers had sung these words they would make a little pause and then they would go on with them. Lusmore knew now that the music came from inside the rath, and he knew well enough that it was the Good People he was listening to. He kept very quiet and listened, and it seemed a wonderfully sweet song to him, only after a while he got tired of hearing no other words. And he thought: 'Maybe they'd like the song better themselves if there was more of it, and I wonder couldn't I help them with it.

"But he knew he must not disturb the Good People, so he waited till one of the little pauses, and then he sang very softly: 'Augus da Cadine.'

"Then he kept on singing all the words, along with the singers inside the rath, adding on his own new line every time:

Da Luan, da Mort,
Da Luan, da Mort,
Da Luan, da Mort,
Augus da Cadine.

"And that means: 'Monday, Tuesday, Monday, Tuesday, Monday, Tuesday, and Wednesday too.'

"As he went on he sang a little louder and a little louder, till by and by the Good People in the rath began to listen to hear who or what it was that was singing their song with them, and then they caught the line that Lusmore had added. Then they were so pleased that they scarcely knew what to do, for they were more tired of the song than he was, only they did not know what to do to make it any better. And when they found it was somebody

outside the rath that was singing it and was making more out of
it than they ever did, they wanted to have him inside as soon as
possible.

"So all at once Lusmore saw a door open in the rath, close
beside him, and a great light streaming out, and then there was
the sound of wings all around him, and next he saw the forms of
the Good People pouring out and flying and whirling around
him like a swarm of butterflies. They caught him up and carried
him inside the rath, so lightly that he could not tell what was
holding him, and he felt as if he was floating in the air. He was a
little frightened at first, but when they had him inside the rath
they set him up above all the musicians and thanked him for
mending their song, and did him all sorts of honor.

"Then he saw some of the Good People talking together in a
little group, and presently they came up to him, and one of them
said: 'Lusmore, we've been thinking what will we do for you as a
reward for mending our song, and we've decided to ask yourself
what it is that you'ld rather we'ld give you. Think, now, what it is
that you'ld rather have than anything else in the world.'

"'It's obliged to you I am for your kindness, gentlemen,' said
Lusmore, 'but if you'ld do what would please me most in all the
world, it's not giving me anything you'ld be, but taking something from me, and that's this hump that I have on my back.'

"'That's easy done,' said the one of them that had spoken before; 'come on now and dance with us.'

"Well, Lusmore, being crooked the way he was, and always
weak, had never danced before in his life, and he never thought
he could; but when they took hold of him on both sides and led
him out, he found that he was dancing with the best of them, and
he felt so light and he moved so easily that it seemed to him as if
he was no more than a feather that the wind was blowing about.
Then one of the Good People said to him, 'Lusmore, where is
your hump now?'

"And he felt behind him for it, and it was not on his back at
all. 'Look down on the floor,' said the one that had spoken to him,

117

again. And he looked down, and there was his hump, lying on the floor before him.

"Then they all began dancing again and Lusmore with them, till he felt tired and then dizzy, and then he fell to the ground, and he knew nothing more till he awoke in the morning and found himself lying on the ground outside the rath, where he had sat down to rest the night before. The first thing he thought was that it was a dream that he had had, but he never had felt so well and so strong in his life as he did that minute. So he put his hand behind him, and there was no hump there. And, what was more, he had on a new suit of clothes that the Good People had given him. Then he went home and told his neighbors what had happened to him, and they could scarcely believe it. But everyone knew that there were Good People in that rath, and there was himself, too, the same boy as before, only without the hump, and so, at long last, they had to believe the whole story.

"Well, the news of Lusmore's wonderful cure was told all through the country, and at last it came to a place a long way off, where there was another boy lived that had a hump on his back. And a different sort of boy he was from Lusmore. His temper was as bad as his body. He was ill-natured and spiteful and lazy, and he would always rather be making trouble than saving it. So when his mother heard the way Lusmore had had the hump taken off him, she thought maybe her boy could get rid of his own in the same way.

"With that she set off with the boy and a neighbor of hers, and they came to where Lusmore lived, and asked him would he tell them all about how it was that he had the hump taken off him. And he went over it all with them and told them everything that he did and everything that happened to him. And in the end he went with them to show them the very spot where he had sat down beside the rath, and there they left the little hunchback, and told him to do everything just as Lusmore had done it.

"He sat there listening for a long time and heard nothing, and so at last he went to sleep, and then all at once he was awakened by hearing the Good People singing in the rath. And they

were singing much better now than when Lusmore heard them
first, for they had the song now as he had improved it for them,
and they were singing:

Da Luan, da Mort,
Da Luan, da Mort,
Da Luan, da Mort,
Augus da Cadine.

"And as soon as he heard it the little fellow, not waiting for
time or tune, shouted out: 'Augus da Hena.' And if it was all put
together right that would make it mean: 'Monday, Tuesday, Monday, Tuesday, Monday, Tuesday, and Wednesday too, and
Thursday too.' Only he didn't trouble to put it together right, but
just bawled it out any way.

"Then the music stopped all at once, and he heard the people
inside the rath shouting: 'Who is spoiling our tune? Who is spoiling our tune?' and out they all came and caught him up and hurried him inside the rath so that the breath nearly went out of his
body. And one of them shouted: 'What shall we do to him for
spoiling our tune?' and another said: 'Ask him what he wants us
to do for him!' and another said: 'What do you want from us,
anyway?'

"And he just found breath enough to say: 'I want the same
that Lusmore had,' meaning by that he wanted them to reward
him the same way they did Lusmore.

"But one of the Good People shouted: 'You'll get what Lusmore had, then; it was a hump on the back that Lusmore had, and
we took it off him, but we don't want it and it's easy to give it to
you. Be lively there now, some of you, and hand that hump down
here.'

"And then some of the Good People got Lusmore's hump,
that was hanging up under the roof, and they clapped it on his
back, on the top of his own, and then they threw him out of the
rath. And there his mother found him in the morning, more dead
than alive and with a hump twice as big as before."

"A fine story that is, Mrs. O'Brien," Terence said, when the old woman had finished. "And why didn't the one of them get the same reward as the other? Sure he did the same as the other in lengthening the song for the fairies, didn't he?"

"He did the same in a way," Mrs. O'Brien answered, "but not for the same reason. Lusmore helped them with the song because he thought they might be the better for his help, and that was all the reason. And he did it in a way that wouldn't disturb them. But the other did it only to help himself, because he thought that he'ld get a great reward for it, and he had no real wish to do them any kindness. Don't you see the difference between the two of them?"

"Stuff!" said Terence.

VIII.
THE STARS IN THE WATER

This is to be another sort of chapter altogether. I am going to tell you now what happened. The eighteen years are gone now and we have come to the time when there is something to tell.

When those eighteen years began, you know, Kathleen and Terence were not much more than born. So, if you have got as far as addition and can add eighteen to nothing and find that it makes eighteen, you will see that by this time they were about eighteen years old. John O'Brien and his mother and Kathleen did not live on the east side of Central Park any more. John had got on better and better with the work that he was doing. After a while, instead of having to do work of common kinds any more, he had been put in charge of other men who were doing it. After another while he learned so much about the work and how it was done and how it ought to be done, that he was made one of the partners in the company that did it. So he got a good deal more money and he was able to take his mother and Kathleen out of the little tenement where she was born, and to live in a better place. Then he had a house of his own, over on the west side of the Park, and it was there that Kathleen lived when she was eighteen years old.

Peter had not got along so well. John himself employed him, but Peter knew enough to go only just so far, and there he stuck. He lived in a little better place than he did at first, but he could never make his way like John. And then Terence, as he grew up, made a good deal of trouble. He never would learn anything useful and he never would do anything useful. He never helped his father at all, and always his father had to help him. If there was any fight or any accident or anything troublesome or wrong within a mile, Terence was always in the midst of it. He was constantly getting his head and his ribs broken, and Peter was always having to pay for other people's things that he had broken, from their heads to their windows.

Ellen's excuse for him, that he was never well and had never been quite himself since he was born, was pretty well worn out.

For, people said, he had always been exactly the same ever since he was born, and if that same was not himself, who was it? But Ellen kept saying it none the less. Many a time Mrs. O'Brien tried to make her believe that the boy was a changeling, and not her child at all, and many a time she begged Ellen to let her only try a charm to see if he was, but Ellen never would hear of it. She always said what she had said at first, that nobody knew him but her. She saw him better when she dreamed about him, for then she saw him as he really was, without all the harm that had been done to him by all the sickness that had been on him one time and another.

You might suppose that anybody who could play the fiddle as well as Terence need not have any trouble in making his own living. He might have found a place in a theatre, like the man whose fiddle he had played on first. He might have taught others to play. Or he might have played all by himself, and hundreds of people would have paid to hear him. But he would play only when he chose, and he would never do anything useful with his fiddle. And everybody said he played so wonderfully — everybody except Kathleen.

And this brings us back to Kathleen. Terence heard before he was many years old something about the plan that Peter and John had made, that he and Kathleen should be married when they grew up, if they both liked the plan. He seemed to forget all about this last part, "if they both liked the plan." He liked the plan himself and he seemed to think that that was enough. He had talked about it to Kathleen many times, before they were both eighteen years old, and it troubled Kathleen so that she tried never to see Terence when she could possibly help it. She had always disliked him, though she had always tried not to show it; but as they got a little older and she found that there was no other way to keep away from him at all, she had to tell him so.

But do you suppose that made any difference with Terence? Well, it did make a difference with him, but he did not let anybody see that it did. When Kathleen told him for the first time that she did not like him at all, he went away by himself. He went straight to the hill that is in the north end of the Park, and there he threw himself down on his face on the grass. For hours he lay there, trembling and crying, and beating the ground with his feet and his fists. And it would take another book as large as this to tell all that he was saying to himself or to the grass, or to something under the grass — how can I tell? And you would not want to read the book. It is not likely that you will ever see anybody in such a rage as he was in. But at the end of it he stood up and looked just as he usually did, and went straight to the O'Briens' and stayed all the evening and kept as near Kathleen as he could, and stared at her all the time. And he talked to her then and afterward, just as if she had told him that she liked him better than anybody else that she knew.

So Kathleen had to go to her grandmother, as she always did when she was in any trouble, and tell her all about it. And her grandmother told her that she and Terence were both a good deal too young to think of anything of the sort, and that she would do all that she could to help her. But she could not do much. She told John about it, and he said that he should be sorry if the plan that he and Peter had made could not be carried out, but he would forbid it himself, as long as Terence was so lazy and so worthless and so bad as he was now. When he got a little older, he hoped that everything would be better, and there was no hurry about anything.

And though Terence made her so much trouble, Kathleen had many other things to think about. She went to school and learned a great deal, and her grandmother taught her a great deal more. Her grandmother told her stories still, and, though she was nearly eighteen and felt that she was getting so dreadfully old, she still liked stories. Then she had a good many friends, and she spent much of her time with them. She visited Ellen often, too, going to see her at times when she thought that Terence would not be at home. Ellen and Peter still lived on the east side of the Park, and some of her friends lived there, too, so that Kathleen often walked through the north end of the Park, near that hill that I have told you about so many times before.

Kathleen was fond of this part of the Park, as everybody is who knows it. But especially she was fond of one little spot that

123

nobody else seemed to notice much. So Kathleen got a feeling that
this one place belonged to her, and she was all the more fond of it
because of that. It was a tiny little basin of water, near the path,
but up a grassy bank. On the side toward the path it was all open,
but on the other side there were rocks, and out of a little cleft in
the rocks ran a bit of a stream of water that fed the little basin.
Then, around the rocks and over them there was more grass, and
the hill rose at both sides and above. On the edge of the hill, right
over the basin, was a pine-tree, and around it were other trees.
Their branches came together over the water and almost shut out
the sky from it, but not quite.

Every time that Kathleen passed it, she went up the bank
and looked into the still water. She had a feeling that if she ever
went by and did not do this the water would miss her and would
feel hurt. When she did this by daylight and in summer, if she
stood up and looked into the water, she could see a patch of
branches and green leaves and blue sky through them, about as
big as the basin itself, and that was scarcely larger than a fair-
sized tub. But if she stooped down close to the water and looked
into it, she saw that there was a great deal of sky under it, below
the trees, which grew upside down. There was almost as much
sky under the water as she could see above it, and she believed
that there would prove to be quite as much if she could only get
her head where she could see it.

She used to look in at night sometimes, too, and try to see if
there were any stars in that sky; but in the summer she never
could see any, because the leaves on the trees were so thick that
they almost hid the sky, and they seemed to be thicker and to
hide the sky more by night than they did by day. In the winter it
was different. Then there were no leaves, but only branches and
twigs, which covered the sky like lace work, and through these
Kathleen sometimes thought that she could see a star or two in
the water, but she was seldom quite sure. Yet she never passed
the place without looking in it, to see the green leaves and the
blue sky or the black leaves and the almost black sky, or the stars,
if she could find any.

On a certain day — the last day of April it was — there was a good deal of excitement in the fairy palace under the hill. The reason of it was that a new fairy had come to live there. Perhaps you never heard of a baby fairy. I have read a good many stories about fairies that said nothing about any such thing. Now, you needn't try to be so bright about it and say that of course there must be baby fairies, or there could not be any grown-up fairies. That isn't so at all. Fairies are not like men about growing old and dying and other fairies taking their places. I have heard of a fairy funeral, but I can't imagine how it happened, and I think that the story about it must have been a mistake. If you have read this book as far as here, you know that most fairies are thousands of years old, and you know, too — for Naggeneen has told you — what is likely to become of them in the end. Still, there is no sort of doubt that now and then a new fairy is born, and there was one born on this day. He was the son of the King and the Queen, and you can guess well enough that a fairy prince is a person of some consequence.

"What will we do at all for a nurse for the baby?" said the Queen.

"What will we do at all?" said the King.

"It never would do for me to have the care of him at the first," said the Queen.

"Never a bit," said the King; "it would ruin him."

"How would it ruin him?" said the Queen.

"Never a know I know, no more nor you," said the King, "but you know as well as I it would ruin him."

"Why can't I care for my own child?" said the Queen, "the same as a human mother does?"

"I dunno," said the King, "only we know you can't. We've never dared try, to see what would happen. He must have a human nurse. Maybe it's something to do with them things Naggeneen was always talking about our having no souls — "

"Don't be talking about Naggeneen," said the Queen, "and me not well at all." Then she was silent for a little while and then she went on talking about Naggeneen herself. "Are you sorry he left us?"

"Who?" said the King.

"Naggeneen," said the Queen.

"I'm not sorry," said the King. "We've more peace without him. Though he was clever and he often told us the right thing to do and he might tell us the right thing to do now."

"Did he tell us the right thing to do when he told us to bring Terence here to learn the ways of men and to teach them to us?"

"Sure Terence is a good boy," said the King, "and he plays the fiddle as well as Naggeneen himself, so we don't miss Naggeneen for the only thing that he was good for. And Terence is easier to have about other ways."

"But has he ever learned the ways of men and taught them to us?" the Queen asked.

The King was getting annoyed. "He has learned them, I think," he said, "but he has never taught them to us. And you know Naggeneen himself said the plan would be no use."

"He did," said the Queen; "only you would try it. And just so all this talk is no use. What will we do for a nurse for the baby?"

"We'll find one some way," the King answered. "Was you thinking of anyone in particular?"

"I was not thinking of anyone in particular."

"How would Kathleen O'Brien do, do you think?" the King asked.

"I don't want to be troubling the O'Briens," the Queen said, "and they always so kind to us."

"It would not be troubling them much; we'ld only keep her a little while and they'ld hardly miss her "

"If she was once here," said the Queen, "some one of your men would want to keep her, and it would break the heart of her grandmother. So it would her father's, too, but I'm not thinking so much of him."

"We'll not keep her," said the King, "only as long as the child needs her."

"You say that now," said the Queen; "it would be different if she was once here — I'ld like to have her as well as anyone I know."

"We could find no one else so good," said the King. "It's May Eve, you mind. There's no time when we have more power, and few when we have so much. We'll all be dancing to-night, and Kathleen often passes along just about dark. It's likely we could get her to dance with us, and then we'ld be sure enough of her. If that fails, there's other ways. Our power lasts till sunrise."

"And you think we'ld not be keeping her long?" said the Queen.

"We'ld have her home almost before she was missed," the King answered.

"I wouldn't mind if you tried," said the Queen.

Kathleen had been to visit Ellen. She was on her way home through the Park, and she had meant to get there before dark, but it was a little later than she had thought, and she saw the red in the sky before her getting darker and duller every minute. As she walked along she saw two other girls of about her own age, whom she knew, in front of her. She overtook them and the three walked on together, though the others could scarcely keep up, Kathleen hurried so.

When they were nearly through the Park they came to the little basin where the water ran down out of the rock. Though she wanted to get home so quickly, she could not pass this place without going up the bank and looking into the water, because she felt so sure that if she did not the water would miss her and feel hurt. She ran up the bank and looked into the still little pool.

The other girls went on, and she heard one of them call after her: "Thought you were in a hurry!"

Kathleen did not mind them, but only looked into the water, which was almost black, it was getting so dark all around. She had not seen the water look so dark in a long time. She looked up over her head and she saw that it was because the little new leaves had begun to come out on the trees and were beginning to hide the sky. She saw one or two of the brightest stars, that had already come out in the sky, and she looked back into the water and tried to see them there, but she could not find them. There was nothing but the little, still, black pool.

She went back to the path and ran on after the other girls. She saw them walking on slowly, only a little way ahead of her. Just as she had nearly come up with them she stood still to look at a wonderful sight. She just thought dimly that it was strange that the other girls were not watching it, too, but the sight itself excited her so that she had not much time to think of that. On the grass, close beside the path, there were ever so many boys and girls — at least she thought at first that they were boys and girls — dancing. The grass in that place sloped upward from the path, and the ground was a little hollowed, in a sort of shell shape. All around the place, except where the path was, trees and bushes hung over the grass. The buds were just opening here, too, and the air was full of the smell of the new spring grass and leaves, which always grows stronger in the evening.

Kathleen stood gazing at the boys and girls dancing. There were so many of them that she could not count them. She thought that they seemed to be a little younger and smaller than herself. The boys all wore green jackets and red caps. When she looked at them more closely she could not tell whether they were boys at all or not. They looked more like old men. And she could scarcely believe that either, because they danced so fast and seemed so lively. Her father could not dance like that, she was sure, and he was not an old man.

But she had no doubt that the girls were girls. Usually she could not tell a pretty girl from an ugly one, any more than any other girl can, but she knew that these were pretty. Anybody would. They had long, golden hair that hung all loose and free and came down to their knees, when the little wind did not blow it away in some other direction. They had deep, soft eyes. They were dressed in long, white gowns, so white that they shone, now like a sheet of pale light and now with a hundred little sparkles, as the water of the sea does sometimes, when it is broken into foam by the prow of a ship. All the men carried lanterns and all the girls had something that looked like long flower-stems, only there were tiny lights on the ends of them, instead of flowers. These and the lanterns did not seem to trouble them at all in dancing, and if Kathleen had seen the lights and had not seen the dancers, she would have thought that they were a swarm of fire-flies.

She had scarcely stood there for a minute before one of the men came up to her and asked her to dance with him. Kathleen's first thought was that she ought to be afraid, and her second thought was that she was not afraid a bit. She liked dancing and she had just been wishing that she could dance with these boys and girls. Then she wondered if it was quite right. Then she could not see what there could be wrong about it. Then she let the little man take her hand and she stepped off the path upon the grass and began to dance. She heard the other girls calling to her again, farther up the path. She called back to them: "I am coming in a minute! Wait for me!" And then she went on dancing.

When she had been only looking on, the dancing had seemed to Kathleen to be quite wonderful, but now she found that she could do it all nearly as well as the little boys and girls. She thought that it might be because the little old man was a bet-ter partner for dancing than she had ever had before. They danced around by themselves, moving in and out among the others, no matter how close together they were, and always find-ing their way, now in the midst of the whole company and now out beyond the very edge of it, and then suddenly all the dancers would join hands and whirl about in a great circle, so fast that Kathleen could not tell whether her feet were touching the ground at all.

It seemed to her that she had never done anything so delightful before. She did not think of going on with the other girls any more. She did not think of getting home early, or of anything but the dancing. She could not tell at all how long she had been dancing, but it was all dark, except for the little lanterns and the little lights on the flower-stems, and the stars were all out in the sky. And then somebody said: "It is time to go."

The man who had been dancing with Kathleen whispered to her: "You are to go with us."

And Kathleen thought of nothing but of going with the queer little old men and the beautiful little girls. They all left the shell-shaped grass-plot and moved along together — Kathleen could scarcely tell even now whether her feet were on the ground or not — over the grass, till they came to a little pool of water — Kathleen's own little pool.

She looked down into it, and there was no doubt about the stars now. There were hundreds of them down under the water, shining up through it from as far below, it seemed, as the stars in the sky were up above. The dancers who came to it first stepped on the surface of the pool, and it bore them up as if it had been a floor of glass. Then Kathleen saw that the rocks behind the pool were not as she had ever seen them before. There was an opening straight into the hill, and when she came nearer still she saw that the water was no longer a little pool. It was more like a long, narrow lake, and it covered the bottom of the opening that led into the hill. All the people were going in, walking along the path of water as easily as if it had been a path of ice.

Again it seemed to Kathleen that she ought to be afraid, and again it seemed to her, still more clearly, that she was not afraid. When she came to the water she put her foot upon it and walked along it as easily as the others were doing. She thought that she would remember that this water could be walked on, and would try it the next day. She had never thought of trying it before.

But now she and the others were moving along the path into the hill. It was still dark, except for the lights that they carried and the stars that shone up through the water. And these were not the reflection of any stars in the sky, for there was no sky to be seen over them now — only rocks. Then there was a pale violet light shining on the walls of the passage ahead of them. Then, as Kathleen looked down at the water again, to see if she were really walking on it, she saw that there were no more stars, but the water was of a faint, shining yellow, and in a moment she was not walking on water any more, but on a floor, that seemed to her to be all of gold.

She could do nothing now but stand still and look around at the wonderful sight. All around her were walls of silver, so bright that they reflected everything in the great hall, and she could not tell at all how large it was. But she made out that in the middle was a great dome, held up by the most wonderful gleaming columns of gold and silver, first a column of gold and then a column of silver, and these she saw again and again in the walls all about. She could not see the top of the dome from where she stood, it was so high, but all around the sides of it she saw great diamonds and rubies and emeralds, some of them as big as her head, that poured down soft white and red and green lights, and these she saw, too, shining up, a little dimmer, from the gold of the floor, which was almost as good a mirror as the walls.

The sides of the dome, in which the jewels were set, were all of bands and lines and ribbons of gold and silver, wonderfully woven together into shapes and patterns which she could not follow or trace out with her eyes, because they seemed to be always slowly moving — turning and twisting and winding and wreathing about, never for a moment the same, but always new and always beautiful. And when this was reflected in the golden floor it was like the wavering shapes in water that is almost still, but yet has little waves that dance and break up every reflection that is seen in it.

And still, although she saw no lamps except the great white and red and green gems, there came from somewhere — perhaps from the top of the dome, she thought — that violet light that she had seen first on the walls of the passage, and it filled the whole hall, like the glow of a glorious sunset that never faded. And all

131

this was inside a hill that Kathleen had known all the years of her life, and she had never seen anything wonderful about it.

*****

While Kathleen is wondering at the fairy palace I will explain to you the subject which you have been wondering about If you only knew more we could get on with the story so much faster. It is most annoying. And you have been brought up so well too! I don't see that it is anybody's fault but your own. You have been wondering all along how it was that the fairies seemed to Kathleen to be, as I said, only a little smaller than herself, when you have always heard that fairies were so very little.

Well, to think of your not understanding that! I am bound to say that when I was of your age I was just as ignorant about it as you are now, but then, children now have a good many more advantages than they had in my day. Considering how few advantages we had, it is a great credit to people of my age that we know anything at all, and, considering how many of them you have, it is a disgrace to you that you do not know everything.

When I was a child I used to read about fairies, and the book would say that they were six inches tall, or that they were about as big as a man's thumb, or it would tell about their sitting in flowers. And then I would look at the pictures and they would appear to be as high as a man's knees, or even higher. And I could not understand it. But I made up my mind to find out about it. That is what you must do, when there is anything that you don't understand. There are very few things that you can't do, if you make up your mind to them, except things that are too hard for you. I hate to have morals getting into a story as much as you do, but that is such a good one that it might as well go in.

Now I will tell you. Fairies can be of any size they like, and you never can tell what size they are going to be, from one minute to another. They can be giants, if they like. And as soon as they had Kathleen with them they could make her of any size they liked too. So as long as she was among them they could keep her and themselves just the same size, or as near to it as they liked.

But when fairies are not taking the trouble to be of any particular size — when they are letting themselves alone, as you might say — then they are about six inches tall. And I think that is a very good size to be. It would be better if you were of that size. You wouldn't eat so much and you wouldn't be so much in the way, and you would be much better-looking. Just think: if your face were only three-quarters of an inch long, all those features of it that are so disagreeable wouldn't show so plainly. You might even look rather pretty. You wouldn't need to be so, but you might look so.

And it would be so much easier to know where you were, if you were of that size, that it would save your mother a good deal of trouble. All she would have to do would be to put you on the mantelpiece, and then you could not get off without breaking your necks — and that would be such an advantage. I don't mean that it would be an advantage to break your necks, because then who would read this book, and why should I take all this trouble to write it? I mean, it would be an advantage that you could not get off. Well, now you see how much better off you would be if you were only six inches tall, and now you understand about the fairies.

*****

While Kathleen was still wondering at the place that she was in, a man whom she had not seen before came up to her. He wore a crown, and she guessed at once that he was some sort of king. It did not surprise her to see a man with a crown. A man with a church steeple on his head would not have surprised her, by this time. "Come with me," he said; "you're wanted at once."

Kathleen followed him to the opposite side of the hall and through a door, into another room. It was much smaller than the hall, but it was just as beautiful, in its own way. There was a woman in this room — another of the beautiful girls, Kathleen would have said — lying on a gold couch. Her hair was hanging down over the pillow on which her head lay, so that Kathleen could scarcely tell which was the hair and which was the gold of the couch. There was a crown lying on a little table beside her, and so Kathleen guessed that she was the Queen. "Kathleen," said the Queen, "do you know why they have brought you here?"

"No, Your Majesty," said Kathleen. She was not a bit frightened, any more than she had been all along, and she knew that that was the way to speak to a queen, just as well as if she had never spoken to anybody else in her life.

"They brought you here, then," said the Queen, "to take care of my baby; but he'll not need you long, and then you can be going back home."

"I'm afraid," Kathleen said, "that I don't know how to take care of a baby very well. I might do something wrong with it. You see my mother died when I was born, and so I was the only baby that there ever was at our house, and I have hardly ever had anything to do with a real live baby."

"You've had something to do with them that was not alive, haven't you?" the Queen asked.

Kathleen smiled a little at that. "There were fifteen of them, I think," she said.

"Well, you'll be having no more trouble with this one," the Queen said, "than with any of those fifteen. Only do as you're told. I can't take care of it myself, because it's the law that it must have a nurse that's a mort — I mean it must have a nurse from outside this place. There's the baby in the cradle there. Try can you make him go to sleep."

Kathleen went to the cradle and looked at the baby. It was wide awake and it stared at her like a little owl. Except for that, it looked like any other baby. The way that the baby stared at her came nearer to making Kathleen afraid than anything that she had seen yet. But she took him out of the cradle, sat down on a low seat that she found, began to rock him gently, and sang an old song that her grandmother used to sing to her and that she had sung to her own fifteen babies many a time.

It was scarcely an instant before the baby was asleep. She put him back into the cradle and then turned to the Queen and said: "Shall I do anything more?"

"Not now," said the King; "come now and have something to eat and drink with us."

The Queen started at this and cried: "No, no!" but Kathleen did not know what she meant. She knew that she was very hungry, and she followed the King out of the room, back into the hall. Tables had been brought into the hall now, and they were all covered with things to eat that looked very good, and the men and women were sitting at the tables, eating and drinking and talking and laughing. They all stood up as the King came in, and waited till he had taken his place at the head of the table, and then they all sat down again, and the eating and drinking and talking and laughing went on.

One of the men led Kathleen to a seat and put something to eat and drink before her. She did not know what it was, but it looked good. She was just going to taste it, when somebody touched her on the shoulder and somebody said: "Don't eat that; don't taste a bit of it."

She looked around and saw a boy — perhaps she would have said a young man — standing behind her. He was very different from all the other men. He did not look old, as they did. She thought that he was of about her own age, and he was taller than she, while all the others were shorter. "Don't eat anything or drink anything that they give you," he said again. "I will give you something to eat."

He sat down beside her and put a little package on the table before them. He opened it and took out some bread and meat, some strawberries, a little flask full of cream, and a larger one full of water. He gave Kathleen a part of all these and kept a part for himself. "I am not sure," Kathleen said, "that I ought to let you talk to me, because, you see, I don't know who you are."

She had let several people talk to her that evening, without knowing who they were, but this boy seemed to be somehow altogether different.

"My name is Terence," he said. "Now I know you are going to ask 'Terence what?' It's Terence nothing; I have no name at all except Terence."

"I know a boy named Terence," Kathleen said, "and I don't like him a bit."

"I hope that won't make any difference about your liking me," said the boy.

"Oh, not at all," said Kathleen. "It isn't his name that I don't like; it's himself. He is only just as old as I am, and he looks — " Kathleen stopped, surprised at herself, for she had not thought of it before. "He looks a little like these men here, who all seem to be so old; and, besides, he isn't nice at all."

"Then let's not talk about him," said the boy. "Will you tell me what your name is?"

"Oh, yes; didn't I tell you? My name is Kathleen O'Brien."

"And must I call you Kathleen or Miss O'Brien? You see you will have to call me by my first name, because it is the only one I have, and so I think you ought to let me call you by your first name."

"But if you have only one name," Kathleen said, "it is your last name just as much as it is your first, so perhaps you ought to call me by my last one."

"Oh, no," Terence answered; "you see my name ought to be a first name, only I haven't any last one, so I think I ought to call you by your first one."

Kathleen did not say that he might, but he afterward did. She thought that it would be better to change the subject. "It's just as if we were at a picnic and had brought our own luncheon, isn't it?" she said. "And all these other people are eating just as if they were at home. Why don't we do the same way they do?"

"Because," Terence said, "we are not like them. We mustn't talk about it aloud. You see they are the Good People, and we are not. I don't know what I am at all, but you are like the people outside. I knew that as soon as I saw you, and I saw that they were going to let you eat their food. I almost wish I had let you do it now — no, I don't wish so, either. It would be mean to let you, and I don't want you to, anyway. You did come from outside, didn't you? Well, then, you must not eat or drink the least bit of anything while you are here, except what I bring you. All that I bring you is from outside. If you eat a crumb or drink a drop of anything that they have here, you can never get out again."

"But they all get out," said Kathleen. "They were all outside when I saw them first."

"Oh, yes," Terence answered, "they are different. They can go out and come in whenever they like; but if anybody from outside eats anything here, he can never go out again. It is that way with me, too, for I am different from the Good People, though I don't know whether I came from outside or not."

"You don't know whether you came from outside or not?"

"No. I came here when I was a little baby. I have often asked them how I came here, but they never would tell me. I have lived here ever since I can remember. Have you a father and a mother?"

"My mother is dead," Kathleen answered; "I have a father."

"Yes," said Terence, as if he were trying to work out a puzzle. "Nearly all the people outside seem to have fathers and mothers. I never had either. I have always lived here, but nobody here is my father or my mother, and I don't know how I came here. I have been here so long, and yet it seems so strange to me. This is my only home, and yet I never feel at home in it. I always feel as if I belonged somewhere else. I see the people outside and I feel as if I belonged with them more than here, yet I have never been outside this place one single night."

"You go out often in the daytime, then?" Kathleen asked.

"Oh, yes; I go out every day, almost, and I go to school. Have you been to school?"

"Why, of course," Kathleen answered; "doesn't everybody have to go to school?"

"These people here never go to school," Terence said. "I am the only one who goes, and then I have to try to teach them what I have learned. Do you go home from school and try to teach your father what you have learned?"

"Why, no, indeed," said Kathleen; "what a funny idea!"

"Sometimes it seems funny to me too," Terence said, "but you see I can't tell whether it is funny or not, because I know so little about the people outside. I don't like to ask them, because they would think it was so strange that I didn't know; but it is different with you. You have come in here, and I can ask you things that I wouldn't ask of people outside."

"If they want to know things," said Kathleen, "why don't they go to school themselves?"

"I don't know that, either," said Terence, "but they seem to expect me to go to school for all of them. I think that is what I am here for. Before I was old enough to go to school at all they used to bring me things to eat from outside, because, you know, if I ate anything of theirs I never could go out. Then as soon as I was old enough to go to school, they sent me, and I came back every night, and they gave me money to buy all my own food outside, and I have done that ever since, and I have never eaten a bit of the Good People's food."

"And don't you like to stay here?" Kathleen asked. "It seems to me a very beautiful place."

"No," said Terence; "they are very kind to me, but I think that I should like to live outside better, and I hope that I shall some time. And then, you see, if I ate anything here I could not go out to go to school, and so I could not teach them. And it is all so strange. It almost makes me cry, it is such a bother sometimes, and then they are so sorry about it themselves and I am so sorry for them, and it almost makes me laugh sometimes, because they can never learn anything. You will see. I think it is time now."

Some of the men were taking away the tables. "It is time for the lesson," the King called out. Some of the other men brought in a big blackboard and set it up. Everybody stopped talking and laughing and stood near the blackboard. Terence made some lines and some letters on the board, with a piece of chalk.

"I shall have to try again," said Terence, "to prove to you the same thing that I tried to prove to you last night. But I'll try a different way, and maybe you'll see it better. Now mind, what I am to prove is this: if any triangle has two sides equal, the angles opposite those sides are also equal."

"And what difference does it make if they're equal or not?" said one of the men who stood near Kathleen.

"Be still there," the King said; "do we want to make telephones or do we not? And sure we can't make telephones without geometry. Hasn't Terence told you that?"

Terence went on: "Let ABC be any triangle in which the sides AB and AC are equal."

"How can it be any triangle, when it's only one triangle?" said another of the men.

"Keep your silly head shut," said the King. "Terence didn't say it was any triangle; he said let it be. Now will you let that triangle be, or will I come over there and make you let it be?"

The man said nothing more and Terence went on: "Now, consider this triangle as two triangles, BAC and CAB."

"How can it be two triangles," another of the men said, "when it's only one triangle?"

"Will you be still there?" the King said. "Terence doesn't say it's two triangles; he says you're to consider it. Will you consider that triangle two triangles, or will I come over there and make you consider it two triangles?"

"I'll consider it seven triangles, if you like, Your Majesty," the man answered, "but I dunno what good it'll do me."

"Then consider it," said the King, "and don't talk about it. Go on, Terence."

"Now, you see that since the sides AB and AC in each triangle are equal, AB and AC in the first are respectively equal to AC and AB in the second, and the angles between these sides are equal. So the two triangles are equal, by previous proposition. And so the angles of one are equal to the angles of the other, where they are opposite the equal sides; that is, the angle ABC is equal to the angle ACB, being opposite the equal sides AC and AB, by the same previous proposition, and that is what I was to prove."

The King looked at the men with triumph in his eye. "There, you blackguards," he said, "do you understand it at all, now that Terence has made it clear to you?"

One by one the men and women began slowly to shake their heads. Not one of them understood it. "Well, Terence," said the King, shaking his own head, "I dunno how it is; nobody could be asking you to make it any clearer than you have, and yet I'm obliged to say there's never a bit of it I understand myself. Maybe to-morrow night you'll be able to make us see it clearer."

Terence had come back to where Kathleen was. "Isn't it funny," he said, "and yet isn't it a pity? I try to teach them as well as I can, but they never can understand at all."

"And do you mean to say," said Kathleen, "that you haven't got any farther in geometry than that? Why, that's only the fifth proposition of the first book."

"Of course I've got farther than that," Terence answered, "but they haven't, and they never will. I have been trying to teach them that proposition — oh, I don't know how long — and they never will learn it in the world. They want to learn to build railways and bridges and all sorts of things, but how can anybody even get ready to build a railway or a bridge till he's got over this bridge and the rest of the geometry? I don't know whether I can ever learn it all myself, but I'm going to the School of Engineering up at the University, next spring, to learn chemistry, and qualitative analysis, and calculus, and analytical mechanics, and graphical statics, and metallurgy, and thermodynamics, and hydraulics, and a lot of other things. But these people here will still be at work on this same triangle years after I am dead, if they have anybody to teach them."

"Now, Terence, my boy," said the King, "there's one thing you can do for us we can understand. Give us a tune out of the fiddle."

Kathleen was startled to hear this boy named Terence asked to play on the fiddle, just as if he had been the other Terence whom she knew. She wondered if he played like the other Terence. She scarcely dared wait to hear, and she felt as if she should like to run away, only she did not know where to run.

But she did not think any more about running after Terence began to play. This was different. And yet in one way it was the same. For the music that Terence was playing was just the music that the other Terence often played and just what most people liked to hear him play best, though Kathleen had always liked it as little as anything else that he did. She had never heard anyone else play it till now. And now it was so different. She could scarcely tell the difference, and yet she could feel it in every clear note that Terence drew out with his bow.

When she was a little girl, almost as long ago as she could remember, she used to say, when the other Terence played this very music, that it did not mean anything. But now it meant something. Meant something! It meant — everything, Kathleen thought, and yet she could not tell at all what it meant. It was not happiness that it meant, and it was not sorrow; it was not merry, and it was not grave. Sometimes it was light and gentle and sweet, and flowed along as if it were a little fountain of music, bubbling and bubbling out of a hidden place; then it would be slower, but fine and firm, and full and free and true. It seemed to Kathleen to mean so much, and yet she could not tell what, except that there was something like a deep longing that went all through it.

And that made her think of the other Terence's music again, for she remembered now, though she had never thought of it before, that there was a longing in his music too. Perhaps she had done wrong, she thought, to say that it did not mean anything. Still, this was so different. If the other Terence's fiddle had ever seemed to be longing for anything, it had seemed to be hopeless, and the fiddle always seemed to be bitterly laughing at those who were listening to it and thinking that it was so fine. She had never thought of anything like this before, but it seemed clear to her now, listening to the same music played so differently. For now, below all the longing and sounding through it, there were strength and hope and life and faith in something good.

I do not say that Kathleen thought all this out while she was listening. She only felt the most of it. But she felt it so much that she scarcely knew what she was doing, and she moved by little and little toward Terence, till she was nearer to him than anybody else, and looked at him as if he were something more wonderful than she had ever seen before, till she found that she could not look at him, because her eyes were wet. And then the music stopped.

Then said the King: "I said that was something that we could understand, Terence, but I dunno if it is. It's the wonderful player you are all out, but I never heard you play like that before, and I think there's something in it that's more than I can find out. That's enough of it for to-night."

Terence had already come back to Kathleen. She could scarcely speak to him even yet. "Who taught you to play like that?" she said.

"I don't quite know," he answered, "whether anybody taught me. They taught me to play here, and the music that I just played is their music, but I don't play it the way they do. I don't know why that is. Just as soon as they had taught me so that I could play at all, I began to play in my own way. Their music is sweet

and bright and merry and sparkling, and sometimes it seems to
be sad, but it never means anything."

Kathleen was startled again to hear Terence say the very
words that she had said so many times about the other Terence's
music. "But I never played before in my life," Terence went on,
"the way I have been playing just now. I think it was because you
were here. You understood, and so I thought of nothing but you
all the time that I was playing, and I think it made me play better.
They never understand. They love music and they hate geometry,
but they understand one just as well as the other."

The King came up to Kathleen and said: "It is time for you to
come and be looking after the child again."

Kathleen went with him and he led her back into the room
where the Queen was. "Where is the box of ointment?" the King
said to the Queen.

"I have it here under my pillow," the Queen answered; "come
here and get it, Kathleen."

The Queen took something from under her pillow and held
it so that Kathleen had to come close to her to get it. "Did you eat
anything?" the Queen asked, as Kathleen bent over her.

Kathleen did not quite know whether she ought to answer or
not, but the Queen looked at her so kindly that she thought that
there could be no harm, and she said: "Only what Terence gave
me."

"That was right," said the Queen, and then she went on,
speaking louder, so that the King could hear: "Take this box of
ointment. In the morning, as soon as the baby is awake, take him
out of the cradle and wash him, and then just touch his eyes with
this ointment; but be careful that you do not touch your own eyes
with it."

Kathleen took the box, which seemed to be of solid gold, and
looked at it. What was in it looked like a soft, green salve. She
slipped it into the pocket of her gown. "How shall I know when it

is morning?" she asked. It seemed to her that here under the hill there would not be much difference between night and day.

"You'll know it's morning when the child wakes up," the Queen said; "or when you wake up yourself, for that matter. You can go to bed now. There's your bed, next to the cradle."

The King left them, and Kathleen, who was really very tired, lay down on another gold couch, almost like the Queen's, that had been placed near the cradle, and in a minute she was asleep.

It seemed scarcely another minute before she was awake again. She remembered that the Queen had said that when she awoke it would be morning, and she looked to see if the baby was awake too. He was, and she took him out of the cradle. Then she saw a large gold basin full of water. She washed the baby in it, and he stared at her all the time, with big, owlish eyes. Then she took the box of ointment out of her pocket. She touched it with her finger and then touched each of the baby's eyes with it. Instantly his eyes looked brighter and deeper, and instead of staring at her stupidly, as they had done before, they seemed to look straight through her. Nothing had frightened her at all, and now she was getting so that nothing startled her. So she only laid the baby back in his cradle and put the box of ointment into her pocket.

In a moment the King came in and said it was time for breakfast. He and the Queen went out into the hall together and Kathleen followed them. As soon as she was in the hall she saw Terence. He was looking for her and they sat down and ate breakfast together. Then Terence went away.

All day, except when it was time for meals, Kathleen sat with the Queen or looked after the baby, though there was really nothing to do for him. Whenever it was time for a meal they went out into the hall, and there Kathleen always found Terence, and she always ate with him, and ate only what he brought her.

In the evening the King came to her and said, "Kathleen, it is time for us to go and dance again; come with us."

Then Terence took her by both hands and said, "Don't go with them; don't go; if you do, I am afraid that you will never come back."

"Of course I shall come back," she said; "you have been very kind to me, and I would come back to see you again, if it was for nothing else. And then I don't know whether I must do anything more for the baby. And then — " Kathleen stopped short as she thought. "I ought not to come back — not to-night! I ought to go home! Oh, how anxious my father and my grandmother must be about me! I have been here all night and all day, and they must think that I am dead. And I have not thought of them the whole time. I am wicked to have stayed here so long."

"Then you will not come back," Terence said. "You know why I brought you all that you have had to eat and to drink. It was so that you might leave this place. I might have let you eat their food, and then you could never leave it, unless to go out with them and dance on their green and then come back again. I made it so that you could go, and now you will go and you will not come back."

"I will come back," Kathleen answered, "but I must see my father and my grandmother and tell them that I am safe. Perhaps I will come back to-morrow, if I can, but I will come back. I would come back just because you wanted to see me, you have been so good to me. It was very good of you, if you wanted me to stay, to bring me the things to eat and drink, so that I could go if I liked."

"No, it was not good of me at all," Terence answered; "I had no right to let them keep you here always, even if I wanted you to be here. But I hoped and I always hope that I shall leave this place some time myself, and I did not want to have to leave you here. I would not have left you here. Promise that you will come back."

"I will come back," Kathleen answered.

"Come along now," said the King, hurrying up to Kathleen again. "It's time we were dancing this minute."

All the little men and women were moving out of the hall and Kathleen went with them. In an instant they were again in the passage that Kathleen remembered. The floor was of gold, like the floor of the hall, and then she saw that she was walking on the water once more. The yellow glow was under it still, but fainter than in the hall. The violet light on the walls of the passage grew dimmer; she saw the lights that the men and women carried, shining ahead of her and all around her. Then she looked down at the water and saw the stars shining up through it, as if there were another sky far down under her feet. And then — she felt the cool, fresh breath of the outside air, and it was delicious to her, and she was standing on her own little pool, and deep down under it there were thousands of stars. She and all the others walked — or drifted, as it seemed to Kathleen — up the bank of sweet-smelling new grass, to the little hollowed place, with the trees and the bushes growing around it and hanging over it, where Kathleen had first seen the Good People. And then they began the dance.

IX.
A YEAR AND A DAY

When Kathleen did not come home at the time she was expected, her father and her grandmother were not much surprised at first. She was in the habit of going where she pleased and of coming back when she pleased. If she chose to be an hour or two late her father or her grandmother might ask her why, or they might not think of it. So, on that May Eve when she danced with the Good People, as it began to get late and still she did not come, they had no doubt that she had decided to make her visit at the Sullivans' a little longer than she had intended. When it got later and still she did not come, her father said that he would walk over to the Sullivans' and come back with her. He never thought of not finding her there. Even when he got there and Ellen told him that Kathleen had gone away hours ago and had said that she was going home, he did not think that any harm could have come to her.

"She met some of the girls that she knew and went with them, maybe," he said, "and she'll be home before me."

But when he got home again and found that she was not there, and when he told his mother that she was not at the Sullivans', they both began to be a little worried. They told each other over and over that Kathleen knew how to take care of herself and that no harm was likely to come to her, but they both doubted their own words. Late at night John went to the Sullivans' again, taking the way that he thought Kathleen would be likely to take, and looking everywhere for her, though he knew that to search for her in such a way as that was nonsense.

The Sullivans had all gone to bed when he got there, but Peter got up and walked back with him, by another way. They went to a police station and asked if there had been any accident — if any girl had been hurt and taken to a hospital. There had been no accident that night. They went home and waited again. At last John could wait no longer. He and Peter started out again and went different ways. They went to other police stations and asked if there had been accidents. There had been one or two, but nobody at all like Kathleen had had anything to do with them. They went to hospitals and asked about all the new patients. There was not one of them that was at all like Kathleen.

It does not belong to the story to tell how they went on searching. All the next day they searched. They tried every way that they knew, and every way that the police knew, and every way that anybody could think of, to find her, and there was no trace. Late that day one of the girls who had walked through the Park with Kathleen came to see her, not knowing that she was lost. Then she told where she had seen Kathleen last. She told how Kathleen had dropped behind the others, though she had said that she wanted to get home early, how they had called to her, how she had answered, and how they had gone on, thinking that she would soon follow.

Then Mrs. O'Brien said to John: "You do not need to search for her any longer. She is with the Good People. I have seen that place often, and it always looked to me like a place where the Good People might be. Last night was May Eve. There is no time in the whole year when the Good People have more power, and especially to carry off young girls. They have taken her with them. Some time she may come back, or some time we may get her back, but it is of no use for you to search for her any more."

But John went on searching still. The next day and for many days he looked for her and tried every means to find her, but she could not be found. Again and again his mother told him that it was of no use, but still he said: "It might be some use, and I wouldn't be easy if I didn't try."

By and by there came a time when even John did not think that there was any use in trying longer. He read many papers, from many different cities, hoping always to find something about some unknown girl who had been found, sick or hurt or helpless, somewhere, but he said little about her. He went on with his old work, and he and his mother were alone and lonely in the house. Then John came to believe that Kathleen was dead. He told his mother this and she answered: "Kathleen is not dead."

"And how do you know that, mother?" John said. "You always say that the Good People took her away, but that might be true, and still she might be dead by now. And the Good People might not have taken her at all. How do you know?"

"I don't know that the Good People took her," she answered, "though I think they did; but I am sure she is not dead."

"And how are you sure, mother?"

"Kathleen could never die," Mrs. O'Brien said, "without I'ld hear the banshee."

"The banshee?" said John. "There's no banshee here. There's banshees only in Ireland."

"Our banshee is here," his mother answered. "I know she is here. You've heard me tell of her. She's the sad, mourning woman of the Good People that weeps and wails about the house when anybody of the family is to die, anywhere in the world. It's true, as you say, that the banshees mostly stay in Ireland, though they are heard to cry and moan for those of the family who are to die in any part of the world. But sometimes the banshee leaves Ireland with the family that she belongs to, and so did ours. Wouldn't I know her voice? Didn't I hear her wail and scream before your father died, so many, many years ago? Oh, I'ld never forget it. I'ld know her voice."

"Then why didn't you hear her," John asked "before Kitty died, and why didn't you know before that she was to die?"

"I did hear the banshee that time," his mother answered, "but I couldn't tell that it was Kitty that was to die. It was the night before she died. I heard a little moan, that was more like the wind than anything else, and then it grew louder, and it was a sob and a soft wail. It did not grow very loud. Then I could hear that it was like the keen that the women cry over the dead at home. I knew that it was the banshee. No, I could not be wrong about her; I had heard her before. But I never thought of Kitty then. I thought: 'I'm an old woman — an old woman — though I would never let them say so; and now my time has come. I shall soon be with him again. If I could only see a child of John's and Kitty's before I go, I'ld go gladly. If I could only say to him: "Before I came to you I held John's and Kitty's child in my arms," then I'ld go gladly.' That was what I said to myself that time. But it was Kitty that the banshee meant. And now, though I felt then the first time that I was an old woman, here I am still, and Kitty is gone and the child is grown up to be a woman and she is lost. But she is not dead, John; she is not dead. Kathleen couldn't die without I'ld hear the banshee."

It was not once only that John and his mother talked together in some such way as this. It was a dozen times at least, perhaps two dozen times, that she told him that, whatever had come to Kathleen, she was not dead — that she could not be dead, because the banshee had not moaned and cried about the house, as she was sure to do before any one of the O'Briens could die. And so John, seeing his mother careworn and anxious, but never so full of sorrow as himself, came to think that he ought to bear it better, and not let her see him always so troubled and so sad. Yet he could not believe all that his mother said quite as she believed it, and she had to tell him all of it again and again, and she told him, too, that when the time came she meant to try to get Kathleen back from the Good People. And after a while John did not think every time that he heard anybody at the door that it was Kathleen at last, and all in the house went on as it had gone before, only that Kathleen was not there. But that "only" was enough, and it was a different house.

The dreadful spring was past; the horrible, dull, anxious summer was gone; the cruel, chilly autumn went by; the cold, dead, heartless winter dragged through; another spring came, cheerless, hopeless, helpless, like the last.

"Shaun," said Mrs. O'Brien, "do you know when it was that Kathleen went away?"

"Could I ever forget?" said John.

"When was it?"

"It was May Eve."

"And what is to-day, John?"

"It's the last day of April," John answered; "it's a year this night she's been away. Could I forget it? Don't I think of it all the time?"

"There's no time in the year," Mrs. O'Brien said, "when the Good People have more power than on May Eve."

"Oh, mother," said John, "don't talk to me of the Good People; I've heard too much of them. I don't care if there are any Good People or not. I only know that Kathleen has been from us a year. When her mother died I could bear it, because I had Kathleen left, but now she's gone, and how can I bear it?"

"Listen to me, John," his mother went on. "It's on May Eve, as I told you, that the Good People have great power. It's then that they dance, and then they make young girls or young men that they want come and dance with them, and then they carry them off. But it's on May Eve, too, sometimes, that they can be got back by those who know what to do. And so it's to-night that we must try to get Kathleen back. I wouldn't tell you till the time came, for fear you might hope too much. We may not find her, and then we may, and you must come with us, for we don't know how much help we'll need."

"Who is it that I must come with?" John asked.

"With me and with the girls that were with Kathleen that night and saw her last."

"How do we know that they can come?" said John. "It's late in the day now and they may be away from home."

"I've taken care of all that," Mrs. O'Brien said; "they'll be here in a little while to go with us."

In a little while the girls came. Then they and Mrs. O'Brien and John went together to the place where Kathleen had met the girls, on her way home from the Sullivans', a year ago. "Was it about this time of the day," Mrs. O'Brien asked, "that you met Kathleen here a year ago to-night?"

"It was," one of the girls said, "about this time."

"Then you must take us," Mrs. O Brien went on, "just the way that you went, and show us the very place where Kathleen stood, the last instant that you saw her."

They all walked along through the Park, the girls leading the way. "How can they find the very place again?" said John. "It's been a year since then. It's likely they have forgot the spot. How could they remember it so long?"

"John," said his mother, "will you never trust me? Do you think that I've been waiting for them to forget all this time? The very evening after Kathleen was lost they brought me here and then took me to the very spot where they saw her last. They talked of it between themselves and decided just where it was, and many a time since they've been with me here, so that they could not forget it."

In a few minutes the girls stopped. "This is the place where we saw her last," they said; "just here. She stood here and seemed to be looking at something there on the grass."

Mrs. O'Brien whispered: "Stand still here, all of you, and do not speak or stir unless I call to you; then do whatever I tell you, and do it quickly."

Mrs. O'Brien drew out something which was hung about her neck, by a chain, under her gown. She held it before her in her hand. She stepped upon the grass and looked all around her. She went a few steps forward and looked around again. She went a little to the left, then a little more to the right. And then, to those who were watching, it seemed as if she saw something, though they could see nothing but her. For she made a few hurried steps and then put out her left hand, as if to take hold of something. Then they saw her raise her right hand, as if to touch the something that she had taken hold of, with what she held in it. Still they could see nothing except her, but now she hurried toward them, and suddenly they saw that she was leading Kathleen, with her left arm around her and holding her right hand against her forehead.

"Take her and go home with her," she said to John, "as quickly as you can. The rest of us will follow."

"Oh, father," said Kathleen, "I am so glad that you came to meet me! Have you and grandmother been worried about me all day? I was afraid you would be, but the baby needed me, and I couldn't send any word to you. And I promised Terence that I would come back — not Terence Sullivan, but the Terence that lives in there. Please ask some of the Good People to tell him that I will come back to-morrow. Then I will go home with you."

"Take her home! Take her home!" her grandmother cried. And John led her away as fast as he could, while the rest followed.

No one said anything more till they were at home, for it was only a little way. Kathleen scarcely looked at her father till they came into the house, where it was light. "Why, father," she said, "what makes you look so queer? You look so much older than you did yesterday, and you — oh, I am afraid you were dreadfully worried about me. I didn't think you would be — such a little while. I forgot that you would be worried. There was so much to see there, and then I had to take care of the baby — and so I forgot. It was very wrong for me to forget, and I am so sorry you were anxious about me. But I thought of you and grandmother just as we were coming out to dance to-night, and as soon as we were done dancing I was coming home. And why were you all there where we were dancing? Did you think that I would be there? You ought not to have been afraid, father. It was just such a little while."

John did not seem to think anything about its being wrong for Kathleen to forget. He did not seem to think of anything but that she had come back. "Just a little while, do you call it?" he said. "Do you call a year a little while for you to be away from me, Kathleen? And from your grandmother? Don't you see how she has worried about you, too, all this long year? And what could I think but that you was dead? Your grandmother never thought so, but I could think nothing else."

153

"A year!" Kathleen cried. "What do you mean, father? What do you mean? Oh, grandmother, is there anything wrong? Has he been sick? What is it?"

"Be quiet, John," said Mrs. O'Brien, "and let me talk with Kathleen. Come here, Kathleen. No, there is nothing wrong, dear. Now listen, and answer what I ask you. When did you see your father and me last before to-night?"

"Why, you know that, grandmother," Kathleen answered. "I saw father yesterday morning, and I saw you yesterday afternoon, when I left you to go to the Sullivans'."

"And where have you been since then?" Mrs. O'Brien asked.

Kathleen closed her eyes and clasped her hands, as she thought of it. "Oh, it was so wonderful!" she said. "I was inside the hill in the Park. I walked right in there on the water with the Good People. And it was so beautiful there — all gold and silver and jewels — and the music — the music that Terence played! And I must go back. I promised him I would."

"And how long were you there?" Mrs. O'Brien asked.

"All the time," Kathleen said; "all night and all day; I didn't go anywhere else. And when it was time for them all to come out to dance to-night — they were dancing, you know, when I first saw them, and they asked me to dance with them, and then I went into the hill with them. And to-night we came out to dance again, and it was only a little while when you came, and then I saw father, and he brought me home. But I was coming home myself as soon as the dancing was over."

"Kathleen," said Mrs. O'Brien, "listen to me now. Don't be frightened, but listen. You've been away from us for a whole year. It was a year ago this night that you danced with the Good People that first time. All this year you have been with them there in the hill. If we had not gone after you to-night, and if I had not known how to bring you back, they would have taken you into the hill for another year, and you might have stayed there, perhaps, as long as you lived."

"But, grandmother! A year! Why, you know it was yesterday!"

"Yesterday was a year ago," her grandmother said. "You can't understand it now. Don't try. You must eat something now, and then you must go to bed. To-morrow I can tell you about it better, and then perhaps you can understand."

But Kathleen could not eat. Her going away had been so strange, her coming back had been so wonderful, and what her grandmother had told her had been so marvelous, that she could think of nothing else. By and by she went to her room. While she was undressing she felt something hard in her pocket. She took it out, and it was the little box of ointment that the Queen had given her to put on the baby's eyes. Now that she was at home again she felt as if she had dreamed all that she had seen and heard while she was away. But she had not dreamed it. Here was this little gold box to prove it. Yet she could not believe it. And they told her that she had been away for a year! What they said must be a dream too. But here was the little gold box, just as the Queen had given it to her. It was a green salve that was in it. She would open it and see if there really was a green salve. If there was, then it was not a dream.

She opened it. There was the green salve. Yes, it was exactly as she remembered it. And she could remember it all so well. She remembered how the Queen had given it to her, and surely that was last night. She remembered how she had touched the baby's eyes with the salve, and how much brighter they had looked after she had done it. Surely it was only this morning that she did that. It seemed to her all so plain. And they said that it had been a year. She could not understand it at all. She laid the little gold box on her bureau, under her glass, and went to bed.

The next morning Kathleen could think about things a little more clearly. She could not remember what she had seen and heard in the hill quite so distinctly. She had not forgotten anything, but it all seemed dimmer in her mind than it had been, as if it were long ago. And still it seemed as if it had all happened yesterday. Everybody whom she knew had heard that she was at home again, and everybody came to see her. And they all told her that she had been away for a year. She could not doubt it any longer, and yet she could not understand it. What had she been doing all that time? She could remember just enough to fill up one night and one day, and that was all. Could it be that she had slept for three hundred and sixty-four days and been awake for only one? No, she could not believe that. And so, at last, she came to her grandmother to ask if she could explain it to her.

"No," the old woman said, "I can't do that. It's too wonderful for any of us to understand. But it's no more wonderful than many things that are true, and I've heard tales of it before. Often one stays in the land of the Good People, and in other places, too, and thinks that the time has been short, when it has been long. Shall I tell you what happened once to a monk — a holy man — much more wonderful than what happened to you?

"One day this monk was in the garden of the monastery where he lived, reading in his book. He was reading in the Psalms, where it says, 'For a thousand years in thy sight are as yesterday, which is past. And as a watch in the night, things that are counted nothing, shall their years be.'

"And he found it hard to believe that even to God Himself a thousand years could seem no more than a day. As he was thinking of this, a bird in a tree near him began to sing, and the song was so beautiful that he forgot the psalm that he had been reading and his thoughts about it, and only listened to the bird. It seemed to him that in all his life he had never heard any music so beautiful.

"But soon the bird flew to another tree, farther from the monastery, and the monk followed, to listen to its song again. Then the bird flew to a tree farther off, and still the monk followed. Once more the bird flew to another tree, and once more the monk followed it, for it seemed to him that as long as that bird sang he could listen to nothing else and could think of nothing else. But he saw that the sun had gone down and he knew that it was time for him to go back to the monastery. As he went back he looked at the colors that the sun had left behind it in the sky, and he thought that they were as beautiful to see as the voice of the bird was to hear.

"They were all faded and the darkness had come on when he reached the monastery and went in. And if he had wondered at the song of the bird and at the colors in the sky, he wondered yet more when he found himself again in the place where he had lived for many years. For many things about the place were changed, and the men in it were all changed. There was not one face among them that he knew. One of the brothers saw him and came toward him, and he said: 'Brother, why have all these changes been made here since this morning? And who are all these whom I do not know? I scarcely know my own monastery.'

"And the other answered: 'Who are you that ask this, and why do you come here? For you wear the dress of our order, but you are a stranger. You speak as if you knew the place, yet I my-self have lived here for fifty years and I have never seen you be-fore.'

"Then the monk told his name and told how he had been at mass in the chapel in the morning and had then gone into the garden to read. And he told how he had read in the Psalms, 'A thousand years in thy sight are as yesterday, which is past,' and how, while he was thinking of these words, he had heard the bird singing. He told how he had followed the bird, till he saw that night was coming, and then had come back to the monastery.

"And the other said: 'I remember now that when I first came into this place they told me of a legend that a monk of your name had gone out of this monastery a hundred and fifty years before, and had never come back and had never been heard of again. And now, counting my own fifty years here, that must have been two hundred years ago.'

"Then the monk said: 'God has given me such happiness as He gives to few until they are with Him in Heaven, for these two hundred years have seemed to me to be only a part of a day. Now hear my confession, for I know that I soon shall die.'

"So the other monk heard his confession, and before midnight he died. And this was the way that God had chosen to show him the meaning of His word."

It was a pretty story, but Kathleen understood no more than before. "No," said her grandmother, "you cannot understand, and I cannot. We live here such a little while and we are so shut in by time, that we cannot understand how it is with those who live always. But we shall understand when the right time comes, and then we shall wonder how we could ever wonder. And I will tell you another story about it, not to make you understand, but to show you how it is.

"Long ago Finn McCool was the great champion of Ireland. He had many warriors, who were called Fenians. He had a son, Oisin, who was a great warrior, too, and besides that a poet and a minstrel. Some of his poems are left to us yet. One day the Fenians were hunting, when they met a beautiful girl riding on a white horse. She called to Oisin, and he went apart from the others to speak with her.

"She told him that she was the Princess of Tir-na-n-Oge, and that she had come to take him there, where she was to be married to him. 'Tir-na-n-Oge' means 'Land of the Young,' and they say that nobody ever grows old there. The Princess was as beautiful as moonlight, and her voice was as sweet as the wind blowing on a harp, and Oisin was in love with her and eager to go before she had done speaking.

"He went back to his father and his companions and bade them farewell. It was with tears that Finn said good-by to Oisin, for I think he knew that he should never see him again. But Oisin did not know. Then Oisin mounted the white horse and set the Princess in front of him, and the horse galloped away toward the west. In a little while they came to the sea, and the horse kept straight on, galloping over the water as if it had been a smooth road. Then some say that the water rose around them and covered them and that they were in a beautiful place under the sea. I am not sure of that. Lands there are under the sea, they say, and

no doubt there are, but I am not so sure that the real Tir-na-n-Oge
is there.

"For others say that the tops of blue hills rose before them,
and changed to green as they came nearer, and then Oisin saw
that soft grass sloped down to the very water here and there, and
in other places there were tall cliffs, and trailing vines hung down
from the tops of them, covered with bright flowers, and they
swung to and fro in the light breeze. Beyond there were more
hills, covered with rich woods. Little veils of mist hid them partly
and made them more beautiful, and streams poured down from
high places and looked like thin, silky tassels hung upon the hills,
and they waved in the air, like the waving vines, and some of
them seemed never to reach the ground at all, but to blow away
into fine silver spray and to mix with the mists of the hills. And
golden sunlight poured down over it all, and there was a warm
shimmer in the air that made it all look like something seen in a
dream. And this was Tir-na-n-Oge.

"The horse came to the shore and galloped over soft turf till
it seemed to Oisin that they were in the very middle of the island,
and there they came to a palace, and Oisin thought that it was
more beautiful than anything else that he had seen. It may be that
the palace was built of marble, but to Oisin it seemed like blocks
of pure snow. It was so long that one might well mount his horse
to go the length of it, instead of walking. It had gilded domes that
looked like suns, with the light shining on them, and the whole
palace was dazzling to look at. All around it were gardens, with
trees and plants in full bloom, of all the colors of the rainbow, and
colors that are not in the rainbow, and other trees with only deep
green leaves, and pathways among them which led down into
cool, shady hollows, with clear brooks running through them
between banks of soft, dark-green moss, sinking their quiet little
song.

"Oisin got down off his horse and then lifted the Princess
down, and they went into the palace. There the Princess's father,
the King of Tir-na-n-Oge, made Oisin welcome and led both of
them to the banquet hall, where a great feast was spread in honor
of the Princess and the new Prince. And Oisin thought that if the

palace was beautiful outside, it was much more beautiful inside, and as for the table that was before him, he could not think of any of the best things in the world to eat and to drink that were not on it.

"The next day the Princess was married to Oisin. For a long time Oisin and the Princess lived in the palace and Oisin thought that he never could be more happy than he was now. The old warriors cared much for what they ate and drank, and Oisin ate and drank better things than he had ever tasted before. He walked with the Princess down through the shady ways among the trees and across the brooks and up the hill-sides among the flowers. They sat together in the garden or in the palace and she sang to him and told him wonderful tales of heroes and of princesses of olden times. Sometimes they rode hunting together, and everywhere they found game, the finest that Oisin had ever seen.

"But at last Oisin began to feel that he cared less for all these things than he had done at first. The grass and the flowers and the woods did not seem so fair to him as they had seemed; the sunshine was not such pure gold; he wished that the silver streams would not blow away in spray and mix with the mists; he wanted to see them come down yellow with the earth of the mountains and plunge into caverns with great rushing and roaring; he felt that the warm air was taking his strength from him; he no longer liked the rich feasts that were spread before him every day; he longed to follow the deer through the woods, with his old friends, to kill it and to cook it and eat it in the woods, and then to sleep there, under the trees and the stars; these trees and these gardens were beautiful, it was true, but they were too beautiful; a hard way through a rough forest would have pleased him better now; he did not love the Princess less, but he longed to see his father and his men again; her singing was no less sweet to him than it had ever been before, but he wished that he could be again where the Fenians, after a hard day's hunt or a hard day's fight, sat about the fire in their stronghold, and listened to one of them — perhaps himself, for he was the best singer of them all — while he sang songs of great heroes and of great fights.

"And one day, when the Princess had been singing to him, he took her harp from her and sang a song of one of his father's battles, a battle which he had seen himself, where Diarmuid had slain hundreds, and Orcur had slain hundreds, and Erin had been kept from her enemies. Then he said to the Princess: 'Do not think that I am ungrateful for all the happiness that I have had here, but I am longing to see Erin again and to see my father and his men. It is not so beautiful a land as this, but it is my own land, and I am longing to see it. The air here is sweet and the sunshine is warm, but I should like to breathe the mists and to feel the chill again, if I could only see Erin once more!'"

Mrs. O'Brien stopped a moment, with the way that she had of seeming to look at things far off. Kathleen said nothing when she paused in this way, and in a minute the old woman went on:

"'You would not be so happy in Erin as you think,' the Princess answered him. 'This is the best place for you to stay, and it would break my heart for you to go.'

"So Oisin said no more then, but the great longing grew upon him, and every day the delights of Tir-na-n-Oge pleased him less. And at last he spoke of it again, and asked the Princess to let him go for a little while. 'You would find Erin changed,' she said, 'and the Fenians are all gone. How long have you been here with me?'

"'I cannot tell you to a day,' Oisin answered, 'but I know that it is weeks since I saw my country and my people.'

"'You have been here,' said the Princess, 'for three hundred years.'

"Oisin could not understand it, but he thought that if he could live so long and not know that the time had passed, the Fenians, too, might be living still, and he begged again to be allowed to go. At last the Princess saw that he would never be happy unless he went, so she brought him the same white horse that had brought them both to Tir-na-n-Oge. 'The horse,' she said, 'will take you to Erin. But you must sit upon his back and never loose his bridle or get down upon the ground. If you touch the ground of Erin you will be at once a weak, old man, you can never come back to Tir-na-n-Oge, you will never see me, and I shall never see you again. Will you promise me, if I will let you go, that you will not get off the horse's back or let go his bridle?'

"Oisin promised and she let him go. Away over the water the horse galloped again. Tir-na-n-Oge, with its warm sun and its sweet air, was left behind. A damp sea-wind came up, and it blew the salt spray harshly into Oisin's face as the horse dashed along. It was a joy to him. No more of the soft comforts of that weary island. This was something for a man to face. Yet he did not forget the Princess, and he meant to go back to her when he had seen his land and his people once more. Then the clouds and the fog drifted away and the sun shone out, but still the salt spray covered him, and he felt stronger as he made his way against it and felt the great, free breeze from the east. And now he saw something like a little cloud on the horizon, and it rose higher and grew wider, and then its misty brown faded away and he saw the beautiful green shores of Erin."

The old woman paused again and said over softly to herself: "The beautiful — beautiful green shores of Erin."

"The horse and the rider soon reached the land now. Oisin rode first to the spot where he had first met the Princess of Tir-na-n-Oge and where he had last seen his father and his companions. He did not think to find them there, but he felt that it was the first place to which he should go. The forest had been cleared away a little, and a strange building stood there. It was a small house, built of stone, and there was a cross on the top of it. Inside he heard a sound of singing. He rode to the door and looked in. There were people kneeling before a man who stood in a higher place than the rest and held up a golden cup.

"This was something that Oisin did not understand, and he rode away, remembering what the Princess had told him, that he would find Ireland changed. He wondered if he had been wise to come at all. But he went on, and now he rode fast, in this direction and in that, to try to find the Fenians. Sometimes he asked people whom he met if they could tell him of his father. Some of them shook their heads and said that they knew no such person as Finn McCool. Others laughed at him. One or two old men told him that the Fenians had all died long ago and that the man of greatest power in Ireland now was Patrick. It was hard for him to believe. He would have thought himself in a dream, but a dream seems right and true while it lasts, and this seemed all wrong and false. Yet, when he found a place that he knew and looked for some familiar stronghold of the Fenians, he found only a low mound of earth, grown all over with grass, or perhaps with weeds and bushes. And everywhere he saw these houses of stone, with crosses on their tops.

"Then it came into his mind to find this Patrick of whom he heard so much, and to see what sort of man was now the greatest in Ireland. This was an easier matter than searching for the Fenians. Everyone knew where the holy Patrick was, and soon Oisin came near the place and found that the saint was building another of the stone houses. As Oisin came near he saw some men trying to lift a heavy stone upon a car, to take it to the new building. It almost made him laugh to see how small and weak the men were. He knew well that he could put the stone on the car alone. It was no larger than the stones that the Fenians used to throw for sport.

"He came near and leaned down from his saddle to lift the stone for the men. He took hold of it and began to raise it, but with the weight the girth of his saddle broke, the saddle slipped around on the horse, Oisin fell, and the horse ran away. Oisin lay there on the ground of Erin, which the Princess had forbidden him to touch, an old man, weak, helpless, blind, hollow-cheeked, wrinkled, white-haired.

"The men took him up and carried him to St. Patrick, who welcomed him kindly and kept him for a while in his own house. Many times the saint talked with him and tried to make him a Christian, but Oisin could think of nothing but the grand days of the Fenians. When St. Patrick talked with him he would begin to tell of these, and he would make the poems about them that have been kept till now and give us what we know of Finn McCool and his heroes. And these poems Patrick would have written down. And always Oisin was mourning for the brave old days of Finn McCool or for the days of Tir-na-n-Oge, which seemed to him now still farther off.

"Old as he was now, with the heavy weight of more than three hundred years upon him, blind and weak, there was one thing in which Oisin felt himself a better man that St. Patrick or any of his band. St. Patrick and all those who were with him fasted much, and when they ate it was frugally, of bread and the herbs of the field, and but little meat. But this was not enough for Oisin. He remembered how he and his fellow-huntsmen used to follow the deer and kill it, and dress it, and cook it on the moor in the fresh, cool evening, and feast till it was time to sleep, and then wake and follow the deer again. And so the food which was given to him in St. Patrick's house seemed poor and scanty to him.

"He said this to the cook and others in the house, and they made sport of him, because so old a man as he should wish to eat so much. Then he told them tales of the days of his father, how great and strong the men of Erin were then, how much more fertile the land was, and of the great beasts and the great trees and plants and vines that it brought forth. In those days, he said, the leg of a lark was as large as a leg of mutton now, a berry of the wild ash was as large as a sheep, and an ivy leaf as broad as a shield.

"They all laughed at him the more when he said these things, and they did not believe a word of it all. 'Alas!' he said, 'how can I show you that what I say is true? The dear heroes whom I knew are all gone. I am left alone to mourn for them, among men who do not even believe how great they were. Everything that I have found is changed, but there may be something that is not changed. Will one of you go with me in a war chariot and drive where I shall tell him, and let me see if I can find anything as I knew it once?'

"Then one of them said that he would go with him. The next morning they set out. Oisin told the man where to drive, till they came to a place where Oisin said: 'Look around you and tell me what you can see on the plain.'

"'I see a stone pillar,' the man answered.

"'Drive the chariot to it,' said Oisin, 'and dig at the foot of the pillar, on the south side of it.'

"The man did as Oisin told him, and when he had dug for a while Oisin asked him if he had found anything. 'There is something long and hard here,' said the man, 'like a wooden pole.'

"'Dig it out,' said Oisin.

"The man dug more. 'I have it out now,' he said; 'it is like a great spear, for it has a huge head of rusty iron. I can scarcely lift it.'

"'It is a spear such as the Fenians used,' said Oisin. 'Dig still deeper.'

"The man dug again. 'Do you find anything more?' said Oisin.

"'I have found a great horn,' the man answered, 'many times as large as any horn that I ever saw.'

"'It is the great war-horn of my father, Finn McCool,' said Oisin. 'Dig deeper.'

"The man dug again and said, 'I have found a lump of bog butter.'

"'Now blow the horn,' said Oisin.

"The man was scarcely able to blow the horn, but he did blow it, and it gave forth a harsh, terrible note, which sounded over the plain and was echoed back from the woods and the rocks with a hoarse, dreadful sound.

"'Look about you,' said Oisin, 'and tell me what you see.'

"'Oh, I see,' said the man, 'a great flock of birds coming toward us, and every one of them is many times as large as the largest eagle that I have ever seen. I fear that we cannot escape them and that they will kill us. The dog is nearly dead with terror and he is trying to break his chain.'

"'Give him a piece of the bog butter,' said Oisin, 'and let him go. Then tell me what he does.'

"'He is running straight toward the birds, the man answered, 'and they are coming straight toward him and toward us, along the ground. Ah! he has caught one of them, and all the rest have flown away! He has killed the bird! He is rushing back to us, with madness in his eyes and his mouth covered with blood and foam! I fear that he will be worse for us than the birds would have been.'

"'Hold the spear straight in front of you as he comes,' said Oisin, 'and let him run upon the point of it and kill him.'

"The man held the spear as Oisin told him, and when the dog came on he was caught upon the point of it, and it went through his heart and he fell dead.

"Then the man went and cut off one of the legs of the bird which had been killed, and they took it with them and started back. As they went they passed a mountain ash which had berries of enormous size, and the man put one of them into the chariot. Then the man saw huge ivy leaves, and he took one of them too. So they went back to St. Patrick's house and showed all the men there what they had brought. The leg of the bird and the berry and the ivy leaf were even larger than Oisin had said. And after that they all believed the stories that Oisin told them, and all of them agreed that a man who had lived in the days when there were such trees and such beasts and such men in Erin should be his own judge as to how much he needed to eat. And so after that all of St. Patrick's men treated him as well as did St. Patrick himself.

"But Oisin died only a little while after that, the last of the great heroes of Erin. He had lived for more than three hundred years, and it seemed to him no more than the life of a young man."

X.
THE IRON CRUCIFIX

Kathleen had not been at home long, of course, before Peter and Ellen came to see her, and Terence came with them. It seemed to Kathleen that she had never seen him look as he did then. She had never seen him look so evil or so crafty or so sad. She felt afraid of him, because he looked so evil and so crafty, and she felt sorry for him, because he looked so sad. She sat in the corner of the room that was farthest from him, and it was also the farthest from all the others, as they were all sitting near together. Then, when all the others were busy talking among themselves, Terence suddenly came and sat close to her, and between her and the others, so that she could not get away from him.

"What did you do all the year that you was inside the hill?" he said.

"I don't know," Kathleen answered; "it seemed only a day to me, and I can't remember and I can't think what it was that I did to fill all that time."

"And how did you like the fairies?" said Terence.

"The Good People? They were very kind to me and I liked them very much, but I wouldn't have let them keep me — I wouldn't have stayed — so long, if I had known."

"You wouldn't have let them? You wouldn't have stayed? And what would you have done?"

"I don't know," said Kathleen.

"And who was there besides the fairies?" Terence asked.

"Why, there was — oh, I don't want to talk to you about it, and I don't think you ought to make me."

"You don't need," said Terence. "I know who was there. I know who he is and what he is, and I know the kind of talk that he talked to you. He made love to you. I know that well enough. That's what he would do. But do you mind the promise that your father made to my father the day after we was born? I want you should remember that promise."

"It was no promise at all," Kathleen said, "and I won't let you talk to me that way, and I don't see that it matters to you what he — what anybody said to me anywhere, and I won't tell you any more."

"Ah!" said Terence; "he did make love to you. And you think you can talk any way you like to me and you won't let me talk any way I like to you. Do you know that his staying in that hill with the fairies depends on me? Do you know that — "

Terence turned to see if anybody else was listening and saw Mrs. O'Brien looking straight at him. He stopped short in what he was saying, and then, speaking lower, he went on: "Don't dare to tell anybody what I was saying to you; you don't know what I can do, but I might show you if I took the notion."

For the rest of the time that he stayed Terence said not a word, but he sat and stared at Kathleen. And now she thought that there was something more terrible in his look than there had been before. It seemed to have a kind of spell about it. Kathleen had a feeling that she could not move while he looked at her, although when she tried it she found that she could.

The most natural thing in the world for Kathleen to do would have been to tell her grandmother about this and about all that Terence had said to her, but, whether it was because of the way that Terence had looked at her or for some other reason, she did not tell her. Sometimes after that, when she and Terence met, he reminded her again of what he called the promise, but oftener he said nothing, or next to nothing, and only looked at her in that same way, and then she felt as if she could do nothing of herself, and that if he told her to do anything, she would have to do it.

Kathleen did not forget the promise which she had made to the other Terence in the hill, that she would come back. She had said that she would come back to-morrow if she could. But when to-morrow came, so many people who had heard that she was at home again came to see her, that she was not left alone for a moment. It was several days before she could get away from the house to go where she pleased alone. Then she went straight to the little pool in the Park.

If you live in New York, perhaps you would like to know just where this pool was — and still is. Well, then — go to the northwest corner of Central Park and go in by the little gate at the right of the carriage-drive. Then you will have to go down a flight of steps. Keep to the right, along the west side of the Park, and you will have to go only a few steps till you come to the pool, which is a little way up the bank, on the left, with the rocks behind it and the trees around it, as I have described it to you before. Then go back to the path and keep on the way that you were going, till you have gone up two short flights of steps. Then, only a few feet farther on, you will see, on the left, the little, shell-shaped, grassy slope where Kathleen danced with the Good People. Seeing these places will prove to you that this whole story is true.

Kathleen went straight to the pool, as I said, never thinking but that, when she got there, she could walk into the hill as easily as she had done before. But there was no opening at all in the rocks. They were just as they had always looked before she went through them with the Good People. Then she tried to step on the water, and instead of stepping on it she stepped into it and wet her foot. She almost concluded that everything had been a dream after all. She felt frightened about it, and she hurried home to look at the little box of green ointment. If she found it where she had left it, it would prove that she had really been inside the hill and that it was not a dream. She ran to her room to look for it, and there it was just as she had left it. It was not a dream.

But how was she to keep her promise to Terence? — the Hill Terence, she called him now, when she thought of him, so as not to confuse him with Terence Sullivan. She went to the pool again and again and tried to find the door in the rocks open and the water so that she could walk on it, but she never found them so. Yet she could not think of any other way to get into the hill again. After a while it seemed so hopeless that she gave up going to the pool so often.

Then one day a thought came to her which made it all seem so simple that she was quite surprised at herself for not thinking of it before. Terence had told her that he came out every day to go to school. He had said that the next year he was to go to the School of Engineering at the University. It was when she first came into the hill that he told her that, and so it was next year now. Now the University was not very far away, up on the hill, beyond the north end of the Park. She did not know whether there was any other way to get into the hill than this way through the rocks behind the pool, but if anybody were at the University and wanted to get into the hill, this would surely be the nearest way. Then she felt sure that if she went to the pool at the right time of the day she should meet Terence when he came out or when he went in.

When she thought again she decided that she would not do anything of the kind. If Terence wanted to see her, it was his business to find her, not hers to find him. After that she thought still more. Terence had no way of finding her. She had never told him where she lived, and he might spend the rest of his life searching for her and never find her. And then she had promised him that she would come back. She had tried so hard to keep that promise already that most people would have said it was right for her to give it up now, but she had a feeling that a promise which she had made to Terence must be kept. She said to herself that it was because he had been so kind to her when she was in the hill.

So she spent all the time she could near the pool, in the hope of seeing Terence. And what do you think happened? She did see him. One afternoon as she was walking along the same old path toward the gate at the corner of the Park, she saw Terence come through that gate and down the steps. And now you will never in the world guess what she did. I suppose you have believed this whole story till now, but I am afraid you will not believe this. I should not believe it myself, if I did not know that it was so. But there is no doubt about it. She turned and walked straight back along the path, and tried to get away without letting Terence see her. Don't expect me to explain it. I don't blame you for being surprised. It was the most wonderful thing I ever heard of. A sensible girl like Kathleen too!

But Terence had seen her and he walked swiftly along the path and overtook her. "What makes you try to get away from me?" he said.

"I don't know," said Kathleen.

"Didn't you want to see me?" he asked.

"Yes," said Kathleen, "I wanted — I don't know — oh, yes, I did want to see you! How is the little Prince?"

"The little Prince is very well," said Terence. "You promised that you would come back, you know."

"Yes," said Kathleen, "and didn't I try? But how could I get through those hard rocks? I don't suppose it was your fault about the rocks, though. How are they getting on with their triangles?"

"They are not getting on at all," Terence answered. "You promised that you would come back, and then, when you saw me you tried to run away. What made you do that?"

"Oh, but I tried so hard to find you!" Kathleen said. "You don't know how hard I tried."

"But what made — ?"

"I don't know; I just couldn't help it."

You notice how uninteresting Terence and Kathleen's conversation was getting. They kept on with it, however, dull as it was. They turned and went up over the hill to the blockhouse, and then down the steep path on the other side and back along the north end of the Park. "Do you come here often?" Terence asked.

"I have been here very often," Kathleen said, "trying to keep my promise to you."

"I am here," he said, "nearly every day, at about this time; will you come again?"

"Yes," Kathleen said, "if you would like me to."

They were close to the pool again now. "See that bright star up there in the west?" said Terence.

Kathleen turned to look at it. "It is Venus," she said. Then she turned back toward where Terence had stood. He was gone. She looked up and down the path and all around, but she could not find him. She went up to the pool. The rocks were just as usual — just as close, just as hard. She tried the water again to see if she could stand on it. She could not. Terence was gone and she went home to think about it.

She thought about it and she thought more about it, but she could not understand it at all. So she very sensibly gave up understanding it. She kept her promise and met Terence again near the pool. And then she met him again and a few times more. Every time he would make her look away from him for a moment, or wait till she did look away, and when she looked back he would be gone. It did not take her long to find out that he did not want her to see him go, of course, and so one day, when she turned her head away she turned it back again quickly, and saw him standing close to the pool with his face toward the rocks. She watched him for a moment while he stood there, and neither of them moved. Then he said, without looking around: "Let me go, Kathleen; I can't go while you're looking."

So she turned away for another instant, and when she looked again he was gone.

I don't know how many times Terence and Kathleen strolled about the Park in this way, or what they talked about, or just how long a time went by, and I suppose that all these things interest you as little as they do me. But there is no doubt that one day, as they were walking together and talking together of whatever they found to talk about, they came face to face with Terence Sullivan. He passed them as if he had not seen them, but his face was black.

The next day he came to see Kathleen, and he said to her: "Do you think I don't know who that was with you in the Park yesterday? And does your father know? He will, if I tell him, and what will he say, do you think, when he knows that you're meeting that fine boy without his knowledge? If I see the two of you there again I'll tell him, and I'll be watching for you too. What do you say to that now?"

"I say nothing to it," Kathleen answered; "what did you think I would say?"

"What did I think you would say? What did I think you could say? Nothing, of course. And is that all you say?"

"That is all," said Kathleen.

And that was all. He tried his best to get her to say more, but she would not. But it did not take her a minute to think what to do. And it was so simple that she wondered why she had never thought of it before. It was a wonder, too, that Terence Sullivan did not think of it himself and know that she would do it. But he was not clever in some ways, though he was so clever in others.

The next day Kathleen met Terence in the Park, and she said to him: "Terence, we must not stay here for a single minute. You must come straight home with me. I want you to see my father and my grandmother."

And Terence went straight home with her and she told her grandmother who he was — and indeed she had told her of him before — and that she had met him in the Park. Her father came soon and Terence was introduced to him too.

After that Terence came often and Kathleen seldom met him in the Park, though they still walked there sometimes. Mrs. O'Brien and John were immensely pleased with him. It was the strangest thing to see how much he liked to be in a house, just because it was a house, and how wonderful the ways of people who lived in a house seemed to him. When he and Kathleen sat together in a corner of the room and John sat reading a paper and Mrs. O'Brien knitting and reading a book at the same time, it was as astonishing a sight to him as it would be to you to see a dozen mermaids playing at the bottom of the sea.

"Isn't it beautiful?" he whispered to Kathleen.

"Isn't what beautiful?" Kathleen asked.

"The way you live here," Terence answered. "All these years, you know, I have just come out of the hill to go to school, and then I have gone back again. I have seen the people outside, but I never was in one of their houses before. And don't you ever dance?"

"Why, of course we do," Kathleen said; "we go to balls sometimes, and to parties where there is dancing, and then — "

"But do you never dance here, where you live?"

"Oh, yes, sometimes we do, but the rooms are not large enough to do it very well, you know."

"I never thought before," said Terence, "of people's not dancing all the time that they were not at work or eating or sleeping. You know there in the hill they dance a good deal of the time, and I get so tired of it that it seems to me as if they danced all the time. I think it is delightful not to dance. And what is your grandmother doing? Is she studying?"

"Why, no, she is only reading."

"But what does she read, if she is not studying?"

"Why, I don't know; a story, maybe, or history, or poetry, or a sermon, or — it might be anything."

"Will you tell me about all those things some time?" Terence asked. "I have heard people tell stories, but I never read a story, and I never read anything except books to help me learn to make railways and telegraphs, so as to teach it to the people in the hill. That is all they think of when they are not dancing."

And Terence wondered like this at everything that he saw, and he often told Kathleen how tired he was of living in the hill and how much he wished that he could live outside among the real people, as he called them, instead of with the Good People. Once Kathleen tried to take Terence to see Peter and Ellen, and then a strange thing was discovered. Terence could not go there. When he came to the corner of the street where Peter and Ellen lived, he turned straight around and walked the other way. "This is the way," Kathleen called, and she hurried back after him.

When she came up with him he turned again and walked with her as they had been going at first. "I don't know why I did that," he said. "I didn't mean to. It was as if my feet turned me around and brought me back."

By this time they were at the corner again, and Terence did just the same thing over. He turned square around and walked back. He could not help it. He tried it again and again and he could not turn that corner. If you had been there and had seen him trying it, you would have thought that it was the funniest sight that you ever saw, though it may not sound so funny to tell about it. Kathleen was vexed that Terence could not go where she wanted him to, but she laughed till she had to sit down on a doorstep and rest.

Terence did not understand it any more than Kathleen did, and afterward he tried it again, but it was of no use. He begged her not to tell her father or her grandmother, because, he said, it would make him look so ridiculous. But one day, when he and Kathleen were on their way together to the O'Briens' house, as he came to the last corner, Terence turned around and walked away. "I can't go home with you to-day," he said. "I don't know why it is. I can't walk that way. It is just the same as when I try to go to the Sullivans'."

He went back to the Park and Kathleen went home alone and found that Peter and Ellen were there. Then she simply could not keep herself from telling her grandmother all about it. Afterward she wished that she had not told her, for her grandmother laughed a little and nodded and looked as if she knew everything, and she would tell nothing.

So the Hill Terence came to the O'Briens' so often that he felt quite at home, and everyone there was glad to have him come, and if he stayed away for as long as three or four days, they wondered what had become of him. And all this, you may suppose, did not improve Terence Sullivan's temper. He and the Hill Terence never met except that one time in the Park, but he knew all about it. And he talked with Kathleen about it sometimes, too, and it made her very uncomfortable. He talked in the same way that he did the day after Kathleen came back from the hill, of his having something to do with the Hill Terence and of the harm that he could do if he chose. He never said anything that Kathleen could understand, but he always made her afraid. She told the Hill Terence about it, and she told her grandmother about it. Her grandmother seemed to understand it perfectly, and she told her not to be afraid. Terence did not seem to understand it at all, and he told her not to be afraid.

Then one day, when Terence Sullivan had been talking to her in the same way and had been looking at her in a more terrible way than ever before, she told her grandmother that she could not bear it any longer. If something could not be done to make Terence stop talking to her so, and looking at her so, she should ask her father to let her go away somewhere.

"There's nothing for you to be afraid of," her grandmother said, "but if you are afraid and if it troubles you so much, we will see what we can do."

Then Mrs. O'Brien went to her own room and came back with something which she gave to Kathleen. It was a little crucifix, made of iron. "It was this," she said, "that I touched you with to bring you out of the circle when you were dancing with the Good People. Hang it around your neck, and if Terence troubles you, hold it up before you and before him. I have always said that Terence was one of the Good People, and I never believed it more than this minute. If he is one of them, he cannot come near the cross, and the iron will be a terror to him too. If he tries to come too near to you, touch him with it, and then we'll see."

"Why can he not come near the cross?" Kathleen asked.

"Because," Mrs. O'Brien said, "the Good People are a kind of spirits, and no spirits can do you any harm if you hold the cross before you, or if you make the sign of the cross. Did I never tell you what the Good People were? They were angels and lived in Heaven once. When Satan and his angels rebelled against God and were driven out of Heaven, the angels that are the Good People were driven out too. They were not good enough to stay in Heaven, and they were not bad enough to fall as Satan and his angels fell, so some of them stayed on the land and some of them stayed in the sea. And so they will live till the Day of Judgment, and then, some say, they will vanish like dew when it dries away; and some say that they will be saved like the souls of Christians. But we do not know."

"You do not know," Kathleen repeated, "if the Good People will be saved or not? They were very good to me, though they kept me away from home so long, and I should like to believe — "

"I have read of one of them," Mrs. O'Brien went on, "who looked in at the gate of Heaven, and an angel told him that he could come in, if he could bring with him the thing which was counted in Heaven the most precious in all the world. And he found it and brought it and went into Heaven. But for the most of them — the Good People themselves do not know whether they are to be saved, and we common people do not know, but they say that priests know. And sometimes the Good People themselves have tried to find out from them.

"There was a troupe of fairies dancing one night on a green near a river, and they were all having the merry kind of time that you know better than I do, Kathleen. But they stopped all at once and ran to hide themselves among the grass and behind leaves and weeds. For they knew, in the way that they have of knowing, that a priest was coming, and the Good People cannot bear to be near a priest.

"The priest who was coming had been on some errand at a long distance from home, and he was a long way from home still. Indeed, he was just making up his mind that, as it was so late, he would not try to go home at all that night, but would ask for a supper and a bed at the first cabin he should come to. And well he knew he would find it and welcome.

"And true for him, close by where the Good People had been dancing, he came to a cabin and knocked at the door. The man and his wife who lived there were proud enough to see the priest in their house and to give him all that he asked, and the trouble that was on them was that they had no more to give. For there was nothing to offer him but potatoes, though they were as good potatoes as there were in Ireland.

"It was only a little while ago that the man of the house had set a net in the river, and he thought that there would hardly be a fish in it so soon. But then he thought that there could be no harm in looking, so down to the river he went to try could he find something for the priest's supper more than the potatoes. And true enough, there in the net was the finest salmon he ever saw. He was about to take him out, when the net was pulled away from him by something that he could not see, and away went the salmon swimming down the river.

"It may be that he said things to the fish that I wouldn't like to be saying after him, and at the same time he looked around to see what it was that was pulling his net. And then he saw the Good People.

"'Give yourself no trouble about the fish,' one of them said to him. 'If you'll only go back to your house and ask the priest one question from us we'll see that he and you have the finest supper that was ever seen.'

"Now the man thought that it was not safe to be talking and making bargains with the Good People, so he said: 'I'll not have anything to do with you at all.' And then he thought neither was it safe to make them angry with him, and so he said again: 'I've no wish to offend you and I thank you for your offer, but I can't take it from you, and I don't think his Reverence would like me to do that same.'

"Then the one that had spoken first said: 'We'll not ask you to take anything you don't want, but will you ask the priest one question for us?"

"'I see no harm in that,' said he, 'for sure he needn't answer it if he doesn't like; but I'll not take your supper.'

"'Then,' said the little man, 'ask him if we are to be saved at the Day of Judgment, like the souls of Christians, and bring us back word what he says, and we'll be grateful to you forever.'

"He went back to his cabin and found his wife and the priest sitting down to supper. 'Your Reverence,' said he, 'might I ask you one question?'

"'And what might that be?' said the priest.

"'Will you tell me,' said he 'will the Good People be saved at the Day of Judgment, the same as Christians?'

"'You never thought of asking that yourself,' the priest said; 'who told you to ask it?'

"'It was the Good People themselves,' said the man, 'and they are down there by the river, waiting for me to tell them what you answer to it.'

"'Go and tell them, then,' said the priest, 'that if they will come here and ask me that or any other question themselves, I will answer them.'

"So he went back and told them what the priest said, and the instant they heard it they all flew away over the grass and up into the air and vanished. Then he went back to eat his potatoes with the priest, still feeling sorry that he had lost the salmon."

"But still I don't see," Kathleen said. "You say that the cross will help me against Terence if he is one of the Good People, because they are a kind of spirits. But why wouldn't it help me against him just as much if he wasn't one of the Good People — if he was just a bad man?"

"No, no," said the old woman; "that little bit of iron will keep you against any evil spirit, and never one of them dare come near it; but no poor human creature with a soul to save, no matter how wicked, was ever turned away from the blessed cross, or ever will be. The cross was made for them. And now, dear, you have been crying and your eyes are all red. Go to your room and try to make them look better. There might be someone to see you before long, and you wouldn't like your eyes to look that way."

Someone did come to see Kathleen before long, but, as it happened, neither she nor her grandmother stayed to see him.

Kathleen scarcely knew that she had been crying till her grandmother told her, but she had. She went to her room and looked in the glass and was surprised to see how red her eyes were. And just at the same instant she saw the little gold box of green ointment, just under the glass, where she had left it, and where it had been ever since that night when she came back from the hill. Then she remembered how the Fairy Queen had given it to her to put on the little Prince's eyes, and how she had done it, and how bright his eyes looked when she touched them with the ointment. She wondered if it would make her eyes look bright, too, and take the marks of the tears away from them. She took a tiny bit of the ointment on her finger and just touched each eye with it. It did make them look brighter; there was no doubt about it.

The next instant Kathleen started away from the mirror and across the room with a little frightened gasp. For, looking in the glass, she had seen a dark form pass behind her, as if it had just come in at the door of the room. She knew who it was without turning around. It was Terence Sullivan. He was still close to the door now, and she was across the room. She had the little iron crucifix in her hand and she turned and faced him.

"What are you doing here?" she said.

Terence only stared at her, for an instant, more surprised than she was herself. Then he stammered: "What — what am I — "

"What are you here for?" said Kathleen. "Why do you follow me like this? I won't let you. Go away."

Terence was a little more himself now. "Which eye do you see me with?" he cried.

"With both eyes, of course," said Kathleen.

"This for both of them, then!" Terence cried, and he struck at Kathleen's eyes with his fist.

She raised her hand quickly to ward off the blow, and Terence's hand touched the iron crucifix. The blow did not reach her eyes. Terence started back from her and fell upon the floor. Only for an instant Kathleen saw his face. His eyes blazed, but the rest of it was as if he had been dead. Somehow he found his way out of the room, Kathleen could scarcely see how. He did not rise, but he seemed to run like a beast running for its life. Kathleen followed him out of the room and to the stairs. She saw him just leaving the house by the door. And yet she could not see how he went, for the door was shut.

Kathleen ran downstairs to find her grandmother and to tell her what had happened. Mrs. O'Brien listened and then she said: "Kathleen, you have been thinking too much about Terence and you have got too nervous. Nobody has come into the house since you left me, only a few minutes ago."

"But I saw him, grandmother," Kathleen answered, "and it was all just as I told you. How could I see him if he did not come?"

Mrs. O'Brien sat and thought for a few minutes. "What did you do before you saw Terence?" she asked.

Kathleen thought for a minute, too, for she was so much excited that she could scarcely remember. "I had been crying," she said, "as you told me, and I put some of the ointment in the little gold box on my eyes to see if it would make them look better."

"It was that," said Mrs. O'Brien. "I've heard the like of it before. When you have touched your eyes with that ointment you can always see the Good People, whether they want you to or not. That was why he tried to strike your eyes, and if he had struck them he would have put them out. You will always see the Good People now wherever you meet them. They don't like to be seen except when they choose, and so they may try to do you harm, and you must be careful. Keep the little cross always by you.

"And now come with me," the old woman went on. "I have had enough of this, and I will have no more."

"Come with you where, grandmother?" Kathleen asked.

"To the Sullivans," the old woman answered.

*****

It was only a little while after they had gone when the Hill Terence came to the door. "Mrs. O'Brien and Miss Kathleen have gone to the Sullivans'," the servant told him.

"Will they be back soon?" he asked.

"I don't think so," the servant said; "it was only a few minutes ago that they went away."

"I will go to the Sullivans' and find them," Terence said.

Now that, you know, was about the most remarkable thing that Terence could say. He had tried to go to the Sullivans' so many times and had found so many times that his feet simply would not take him there, that he had given up trying long ago. But now he resolved that he would go, and, more than that, he had a feeling such as he had never had before that he must go.

He knew the street and the number, though he had never been there. He started off as if there could not be the slightest doubt of his going wherever he wished to go. He walked quickly through the Park and past the little pool as if he had never seen the place. He came out of the Park at the other side and went on till he came to the corner which he could never turn before. He turned it as if it had been any other corner. It did not even surprise him to find that he could. He thought that he was doing all this just because he was so determined to go just where he chose, but he had never felt anything like the force or the determination or whatever it was which was drawing him straight on.

He reached the house and went up the steps. The door was open, and, instead of ringing, he went straight in. But what he did next was the strangest of all. He could not have told you why he did it any more than he could have told you why he did anything else. Instead of knocking at the door or going into any room that he passed, he went downstairs to the door of the kitchen. There, just for one instant, he stopped — the first instant that he had stopped since he left the O'Briens' house. Then, still without knocking, he pushed the door open and went in.

THE OLD KING COMES BACK

When Mrs. O'Brien and Kathleen left home they walked through the Park and to the Sullivans'. Peter was away. Terence half sat and half lay on the floor in a corner. He held his right hand behind him and covered his face with his left arm. His whole body shook as if he were riding in a cart over a rough road. Ellen sat close to him, trying to soothe him and trying to get him to tell her what was the matter.

When Mrs. O'Brien and Kathleen came in Terence seemed to try to make himself smaller, but he did nothing else. "Ellen," said Mrs. O'Brien, "come outside the room here for a moment; I have something to tell you."

"Look at Terence there," Ellen answered; "how can I leave him when he's that way?"

"Leave him," said Mrs. O'Brien, "and come out here with me."

She took Ellen by the hand and led her, and Ellen followed. There was something in Mrs. O'Brien's look now that told her she would have to come. "Now look at me," said Mrs. O'Brien, when they were out of the room; "do I look as if I would mean every word I said, or do I not?"

Ellen did not answer, and Mrs. O'Brien said: "Ellen, when it was only your own affair I told you what you ought to do, but I let you take your own way. But now it is Kathleen's affair and John's and mine, and it is time that I had my way. Look at me, Ellen, and tell me, do I look as if I meant to have it?"

Again Ellen looked in the old woman's face and said nothing for an instant. Then she looked down again in a confused way, and said: "I must go back to Terence."

"Ellen," said the old woman, "go down to the kitchen. We'll follow you, and Terence can come, too, if he likes, and I think he will."

Without a word Ellen went down the stairs. Mrs. O'Brien called to Terence: "We are going to the kitchen; you can come if you like."

Mrs. O'Brien and Kathleen followed Ellen, and Terence followed them. He slipped down the stairs like a bundle of rags. He stole into the kitchen after the others and half sat and half lay in the corner, as he had done in the room above, only he did not cover his face with his arm, but kept his eyes on Mrs. O'Brien to see what she was going to do.

"Now, Ellen," Mrs. O'Brien whispered, "put your largest pot on the fire, put water in it, and let it boil."

Ellen looked at the old woman as if she were begging her not to do this. The old woman looked back at her, and then she did it. She put the pot on the fire and the water in the pot. "Now bring all the eggs you have in the house," Mrs. O'Brien said.

Ellen was past asking questions now, and she brought the eggs. It always takes a long time for water to boil, and it seemed to all of them as if it took hours for this water to boil. While they were waiting not one of them spoke and they scarcely moved. Terence was all but holding his breath, and his eyes, red and staring, were now upon Mrs. O'Brien and now upon Ellen, and never at rest. Kathleen looked at Terence and clutched the little crucifix in her hand. But she need not have been afraid of Terence; he knew the crucifix as well as he cared to know it.

After a long time the water boiled. Mrs. O'Brien waited till it was boiling as hard as ever it could, and then she whispered to Ellen: "Break the eggs now; keep the shells and throw away the rest."

Poor Ellen could not guess what it all meant, but she broke the eggs, laid the shells carefully aside, and threw away the rest.

"Now," said Mrs. O'Brien, "put the shells in the pot."

Ellen did as she was told.

"What are you doing, mother?" Terence called from his corner.

"Tell him you are brewing," Mrs. O'Brien whispered.

"I'm brewing, Terence," said Ellen, scarcely loud enough to be heard.

"And what are you brewing?" Terence asked again.

"Say egg-shells," Mrs. O'Brien whispered.

"Egg-shells, Terence," Ellen said.

Terence sprang to his feet. "Egg-shells!" he cried. "For near six thousand years I have lived on this earth, and never till this minute did I see anybody brew egg-shells!"

Mrs. O'Brien had turned upon him before he had done speaking. "Six thousand years, is it, that you've been on this earth?" she cried. "Then go and spend the rest of the years where you spent the six thousand! You've been long enough here! And send back the child that was stolen when you came here!"

Terence sprang toward a window. Ellen stood in his way; he struck her in the face with his open hand and threw her on the floor. After that nobody saw him but Kathleen. She saw him go toward the window. It was open just a little crack. Before her very eyes he grew smaller and smaller, till he scrambled and rolled and slipped through the crack and was gone.

That very instant the door opened and the Hill Terence came in. He saw Ellen lying on the floor, and, without noticing anyone else, he went to her and lifted her up. Ellen looked in his face, started back from him for an instant, still gazing in his face, and then caught him in her arms and cried, with her voice all full of tears, "It's my own boy — my own boy — the one I always saw in my dreams! Don't come near me, any of you, or you'll wake me and it'll be another dream! Oh, let me keep this dream while I can!"

"You'll keep this dream always, Ellen, dear," the old woman said. "Have no more fear. This is the dream that's for all your life and forever."

It was about that time, or it may have been a little later, that Peter came in. They told him all about it as well as they could. "It's glad I am that it all came out so," Peter said, after they had completely bewildered him by trying to make him understand the story; "it's glad I am. And yet I did like to hear Terence play the fiddle."

"I can play the fiddle a little too," the new Terence said.

"Oh, yes, indeed he can!" said Kathleen. "Bring the fiddle and he will show you."

Peter brought the fiddle and Terence played, and the fiddle sang a great song of gladness — the song of a soul born to find itself a full man all at once.

"Ah! don't you see now? Don't you see now?" Kathleen cried. "That means something!"

*****

The fairies in the hill were dancing their endless dance, when Naggeneen, as if he had been lifted up in the air and dropped, was suddenly among them. They stopped the dance and gathered around him. "What for are you back here?" the King asked.

"They drove me out!" Naggeneen cried. "I knew they would! I told you they would! I told you you could do nothing and I could do nothing! It's the only wonder that they didn't drive me out long ago."

"What do you keep your hand behind you for?" the King asked.

"I couldn't tell you that," said Naggeneen; "I couldn't say the words that I'ld have to say to tell you."

"And how did they drive you out?"

"By brewing egg-shells."

"And do you mean," the King cried, "that you let them catch you with that old trick? I thought you was clever."

"Let them catch me! I couldn't help what they did! I tried to help it, but it's a spell that's too strong for me or for any of us. If I was to get a soul by it, I couldn't help saying: 'What are you doing, mother?' and then I couldn't help saying how long I had been on the earth. Ah, didn't I always tell you mortals was more powerful than us, if they only knew how? What are our spells and our charms to theirs?"

"And where is Terence, then?" the King asked.

"He's not come in yet," somebody answered.

"You know where he must be by this time," said Naggeneen. "He's back with his father and his mother by now. Where else could he be?"

"There'll be no geometry to-night," the King said. "It's all done; we've failed in that. We'll always be as we are, as you told us, Naggeneen. So now be as you were yourself and give us a tune to dance by. We was dancing when you came in, but it was no good music we had."

"I'll not play any more," Naggeneen said; "that's all done too. But I have something more to tell you. Kathleen O'Brien can see us, whether we like it or not. Some fool of you must have given her the ointment when she was here, and now she has used it on her eyes. She saw me when I meant to be invisible, and by the same token she can see any of you any time, whether you want to be seen or not. Now you know it's the rule that she must be blinded in some way. Any of you can do it that likes. I've had enough and I warn you. She carries something that none of you can face, if she uses it. But you can watch your chance and do it when she's asleep or in some way off her guard."

An angry murmur ran around when Naggeneen said this. The King was about to speak, but the Queen spoke first. "Never a one of you shall harm her," she said. "Look what she did for me and the little Prince, at that time when we can do nothing for ourselves. And how good her grandmother has always been to us; and her mother, when she was alive. I don't care if she sees everything we do; no one of us shall ever harm her or anyone that belongs to her."

"You are right," the King said, "and it's ordered as you say.'

"And she's not to be blinded, then?" said Naggeneen.

"She's not to be harmed," the King answered. "I forbid you ever to touch her, Naggeneen, and none of us ever will."

"Don't fear for me," said Naggeneen. "I'll never go near her. I've had enough."

"And we've all had enough," said the King; 'so now, Nag-geneen, play for us."

"Leave me be," said Naggeneen; "I'll never play for you again. King, did you ever lose what you cared for more than all the world? When you do, you'll know more than you know now, with all your age and with all your power. I told you once how I carried off the Princess of France and how Guleesh na Guss Dhu stole her from me. I cared nothing for her. It was only the soul that I'ld get from her that I wanted. And this time it was only the soul that I wanted, too, at first, but I loved this one in the end. But a soul will always find out another soul, and there's nothing for one like us, that has no soul. Oh, I couldn't even tell her like a man. All I could do was to be always frightening her and threat-ening her, and I knew all the time that it would drive her away from me at last, or me away from her. And I'll be like the rest of you till the Last Day, and then it's not even a little smoke that there'll be left of us. Dance and play and do what you like, but leave me be."

Naggeneen turned away from the King, pushed his way through the crowd, and threw himself down in a corner of the hall, with his face against the wall. The rest did not dance any more that night. Naggeneen had frightened them, as he always frightened them when he chose.

After that for a time everything went with the fairies as it had gone at first, except that Naggeneen was not among them. Sometimes he was in the hall by himself and sometimes he was out of it by himself, but he never danced with the others, he never talked with them, and he never played for them.

One day the King came to him as he sat in his corner alone and said, "Naggeneen, we are all going to the wedding. Will you come with us?"

"Leave me be," said Naggeneen. "Why would I want to see it? I don't know if I'll ever go with you or do anything with you again, or with anyone, but I know I'll not now."

All the people who were passing St. Patrick's Cathedral could tell by the looks of things that if they waited long enough they would see somebody come out. So a good many waited. After a while they saw Terence and Kathleen come out and get into a carriage.

"Look," said Kathleen: "do you see them? They are the Good People! Don't you see them all around us, in the street and in the air, and everywhere? I remember every one of them — the funny little men and the pretty little girls. Oh, you goose, you have lived with them all your life, and still you can't see them except when they want you to. But my eyes are different, and I can see them always. Here is one of them coming close to the carriage. It is the King. Yes, Your Majesty. What do you think he says, Terence? He says that they are never going to try to put my eyes out and are never going to do me any harm at all, and that I am never to be afraid of them."

Presently the people who were waiting outside the Cathedral saw John O'Brien and his mother come out and get into another carriage. "Shaun," said the old woman, "I'm wishing that poor Kitty — Heaven rest her soul! — could be here to-day."

"I was thinking that same, mother," said John.

"I think she sees it all," said his mother.

"I think so," said John.

"Shaun," said the old woman again, "isn't it all as well as it could be? Isn't my old King back with us, and isn't it the luck of O'Donoghue that we've found again?"